THE
LAST
RABBIT

THE
LAST
RABBIT

Shelley Moore Thomas

Illustrations by Julie Mellan

WENDY
LAMB
BOOKS

Visit us on the Web! rhcbooks.com

Educators and librarians, for a variety of teaching tools, visit us at RHTeachersLibrarians.com

Library of Congress Cataloging-in-Publication Data
Names: Thomas, Shelley Moore, author.
Title: The last rabbit / Shelley Moore Thomas.
Description: New York : Wendy Lamb Books, [2021] | Audience: Ages 8–12. | Audience: Grades 4–6. | Summary: Albie, an enchanted rabbit who lived on the island of Hybrasil, visits each of her sisters, now living as humans, to decide where she wants to go before the island sinks.
Identifiers: LCCN 2020009571 (print) | LCCN 2020009572 (ebook) | ISBN 978-0-593-17353-4 (hardcover) | ISBN 978-0-593-17354-1 (library binding) | ISBN 978-0-593-17356-5 (trade paperback) | ISBN 978-0-593-17355-8 (ebook)
Subjects: CYAC: Magic—Fiction. | Rabbits—Fiction. | Metamorphosis—Fiction. | Sisters—Fiction. | Fantasy.
Classification: LCC PZ7.T369453 Las 2021 (print) | LCC PZ7.T369453 (ebook) | DDC [Fic]—dc23

The text of this book is set in 12.5-point Bell MT Pro.
Interior design by Michelle Cunningham

Printed in Canada
10 9 8 7 6 5 4 3 2 1
First Edition

For Noel Victoria,
Isabelle Catalina,
and Caledonia Grace

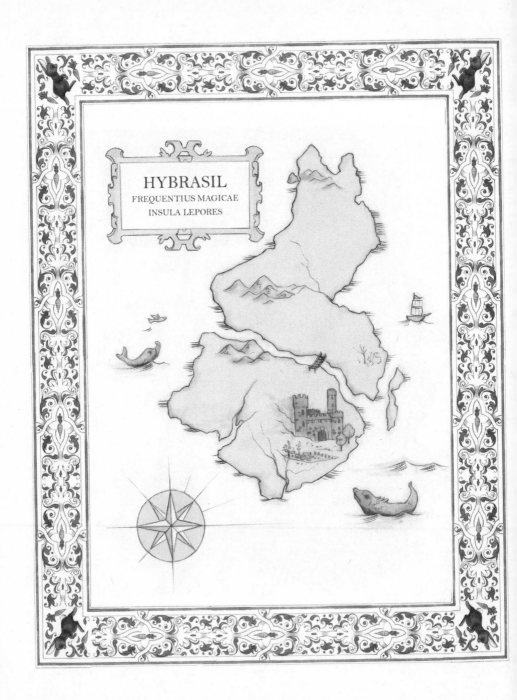

HYBRASIL

FREQUENTIUS MAGICAE

INSULA LEPORES

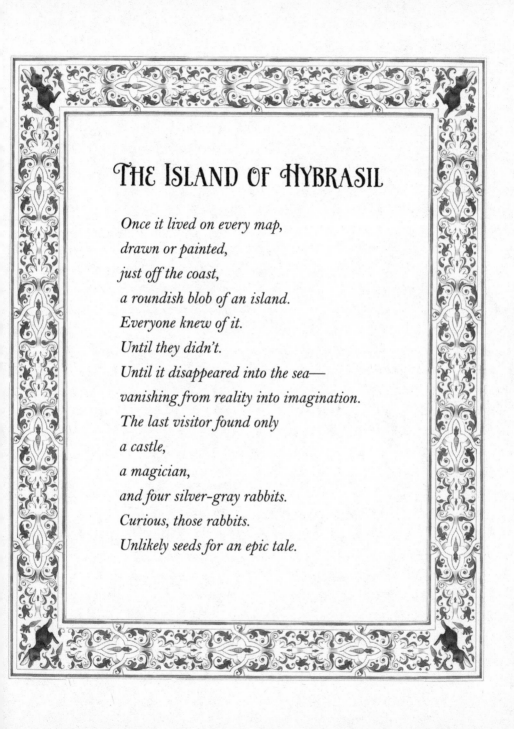

THE ISLAND OF HYBRASIL

Once it lived on every map,
drawn or painted,
just off the coast,
a roundish blob of an island.
Everyone knew of it.
Until they didn't.
Until it disappeared into the sea—
vanishing from reality into imagination.
The last visitor found only
a castle,
a magician,
and four silver-gray rabbits.
Curious, those rabbits.
Unlikely seeds for an epic tale.

Part I

In Which I Am a Rabbit on a Magical Island

Chapter One

I wasn't always a rabbit—that much I can tell you.

Two years ago on this island, there were no rabbits at all. Just four girls, sisters, and a grumpy old man.

Before that, just the grumpy old man.

And then things . . . happened.

If you're guessing that magic was involved, you're correct.

Being a rabbit was not a bad thing, actually. Especially if a person liked carrots, lettuce, and other crispy green things. And fresh peas, perhaps the most perfect food on earth. (Not the kind that come in a tin and look like droppings.) Maybe being a rabbit was even better than being a girl. I had learned to be a good rabbit, after all.

I don't know if I was a very good girl.

Now there were choices to make. If I stayed a rabbit, I could stay with the old man—we called him the

Magician—and find a way to save the island. This was the hope that lulled me to sleep each night and greeted me when I awoke each morning.

If I didn't remain a rabbit . . . well, that created all sorts of new problems. The biggest problem would soon return to the island, with big words like *future* and *destiny* and plans to take me away.

That problem's name was the Boy.

When the Boy arrived, I wasn't in the safety of my burrow. The Magician had planted quite a spring garden of sweet peas and miniature radishes, bless him! I have already spoken of the deliciousness of fresh vegetables, I know, but sometimes once is not enough. Unless there is broccoli in your garden, which I certainly hope there is *not*. Everyone knows broccoli is stupid. Why it even exists, I don't know.

They weren't coming up easily, the radishes. Instead of slithering nicely out of the moist dirt, they hung on to thick glops of mud.

"Ah, Albie, look at your paws—covered in filth. That isn't like you," the Magician said when he spied me radishing. A rabbit enjoys dirt, of course, but mud is another thing altogether. Yuck.

"You see, Albie. It's getting worse," he said. "We're sinking. Soon we'll be knee-deep in mud. And then . . ."

His words dangled.

The Magician sighed deeply, the breath rattling out of his old bones, and he walked back toward the castle.

I was going to need a new burrow—and quick. I'd need a safe place to hide from that wretched Boy. On the other side of the castle was a hill that was still high and dry. It would do nicely.

As I dug my new home and gathered carrots to snack on, I found myself thinking about my old home in Cork and all of the things I loved and missed. I remembered Mum, brushing out the tangles in my hair, whispering kind things in my ear to distract me from the tugging and pulling. "Don't fuss, Albie," she would say. "You are stronger than you know." Or Papa, giving me my first slingshot, teaching me to aim strong and true. He was the one who gave me my nickname, Albie. He said that Alberta was stuffy. Apparently, Mum had picked the name, but I didn't hold that against her.

But other memories were terrible, filled with bombs and explosions.

The very best memories were those of my sisters, but they were also the hardest. I missed them so very much. I clutched my carrots close to my heart. Carrots were everyone's favorite.

A clomping-through-the-mush sound startled me back to reality.

The clomping got louder. I froze, my carrots falling to the ground with a soft thud.

I should've known the Boy would come early.

He wasn't predictable. How such an irresponsible lad got a job as important as rowing *the* boat, I don't understand. But letting my questions niggle around in my brain wasn't doing me any good. I had to find a way out of the garden before he saw me. Or else.

The garden lay between the shore and the old castle. The Boy was going to have to pass through to get to the Magician in the castle. There was no path. We didn't need one, for we didn't have any visitors on this island.

Only the Boy.

"Hulloooooooo," the Boy called from the far side of the garden. As if the Magician could hear him. The Magician was old, getting older all the time. His hearing wasn't that good, which was to my benefit. How else could I sneak into the house whenever I wanted a cup of hot cocoa? And no, I didn't make the cocoa myself. I simply licked the dregs from the bottom of the cup. The Magician drinks tea on the nights he wants to stay up and work on magic and cocoa on the nights he wants to read.

I hid behind a rather large cabbage. Cabbages are better

than broccoli but not much. The old Magician loves to cook colcannon, a potato-cabbage mixture that smells truly noxious. Thus, he grows lots of large cabbages. At this moment, I was quite grateful for mine.

For I wasn't a tiny rabbit. When we were first changed into rabbits, we were small, but soon we became the largish, silverish variety with soft pink on the inside of our ears. Each of us had a distinct marking. Mine is on my tail. There were four of us once. Four beautiful, majestic silver rabbits on the island of Hybrasil.

Now there's only me, on a sinking island.

The Boy was stepping gingerly through the garden. Luckily, the best part of the carrots was still underground,

though I loved to nibble on the lacy green top. I watched, trying not to breathe.

Just then the Boy looked behind him, right at me. Or so it seemed. I was but one more gray shadow on a shadowy day.

"Hulloooooooo?" he called again. He was closer to the old castle now. Close enough for the Magician to hear him.

The Boy turned around quickly.

"I know you're out there. Watching. I can feel it."

I doubted this. From everything I knew of the Boy, he wasn't the sort who could feel things.

"And we both know why I'm here. It's your turn." A chill trailed down my spine.

I froze.

Yes. It was my turn.

"It'll be easier, you know, if you just come with me," he said.

If a rabbit could snort, I would have. It came out as more of a sneeze instead.

"I knew it." He took a small step toward the cabbages. I didn't think he'd be fast enough to get me. Unless he'd been practicing since the last time.

"Ah, my Boy, you've come!" the Magician said from the edge of the garden. The Boy turned, and I skittered back toward the forest and leaped behind a log. I dared not look up, but a rabbit does have fine ears.

The clumping of the Magician's uneven step was getting closer. One of his legs didn't work like the other, and he used a stick to help him along. Perhaps if he'd used his magic on his leg . . .

"The rabbit is nearby, sir," said the Boy. "I feel it."

"You're getting better. Well done, lad," said the Magician. "Yes, she's here. But the task is the same as always. You can't take the rabbit by force. She has to go willingly. Like the others."

The Boy sighed. "I know. I hoped that, being the last, the rules had changed."

The Magician laughed wheezily. "Now, why would the rules change?"

"I thought that with the island sinking more noticeably and all, you'd be more eager to . . . to help."

"You've had an easy time of it so far, with the others. This one, well, she will not be easy."

No. I would not.

"Come inside. I've a fresh batch of colcannon. Fill your belly, lad, and we'll talk strategy. You may ask me your questions as usual."

I chanced a peek over the log. The Boy walked to the castle with shoulders slumping. I hoped it was because he hated colcannon.

It would serve him right.

Chapter Two

It would've been so much easier if the Magician had just told us the rules from the beginning. Instead, we had to piece them together from bits of what he said. This is what I finally determined to be the rules of the magical agreement between himself and the Boy—although I might be wrong about number three. I mean, the world is really, really big.

1. *A rabbit cannot be forced into the boat. She must choose to get on board.*
2. *Only one rabbit at a time may leave.*
3. *The rabbit can choose any place in the world to go, and the Boy must ferry her there.*
4. *Only then can the rabbit change back.*
5. *The rabbits must never know the circumstances behind this agreement.*

My favorite rule was the first one. It was the only thing saving me from being plucked by the ears and plopped onto that stupid boat. My least favorite rule was the last one.

Things that I wasn't supposed to know made me want to find out about them all the more. I'm nosy. Perhaps all rabbits are.

Spying came quite naturally to me, so as the sun faded from the sky, I hopped up next to the window on silent paws. The Magician had dished the Boy a huge bowl of potatoes and limp, cooked cabbage. Disgusting. I wanted to laugh, until the Boy tucked in. He closed his eyes, savoring each bite.

He was putting on quite the show. Then I realized that he was just showing off. He expected me to watch.

Pathetic. I mean it was pathetic that I was actually watching.

"This is good," he said. "But not as good as the food on the mainland. There, they add bacon to the colcannon—"

"We only eat vegetables here, you know that," said the Magician.

"I beg your pardon, sir. I didn't mean to offend." The Boy had manners, at least.

"No offense taken," said the Magician. There were cakes on the table, the small ones with crème filling and chocolate icing on the top. My favorites. The Magician knew this, which is probably why he put them there, to entice me into the open.

Not a chance.

I was spying through the window, with a nice thick pane of wavy glass between us. Easy for me to hear through but not so easy for them to see through. Especially with night falling.

"How are the others?" asked the Magician.

"Fine, last time I checked," said the Boy. "I pass through every few months, you know."

"I would expect no less of you," said the Magician.

The Boy puffed up a bit.

"But this last one, sir, if I may be blunt?"

"Aye. Be as blunt as a knife with no blade."

"This last one, I've watched her the whole time, from when I took the first rabbit, Caragh, across the Sea. She has watched me even more than I watched her. She knows my every move. I fear it will take too long to convince her. I fear we won't make it before—"

"That is preposterous! I know what you imply."

The Magician's face was as red as a tomato. He was quick to temper, a poor quality in a practitioner of magic.

"I'm not implying anything, sir. I just worry for the island. That's all. And maybe I worry a bit for you, too, sir."

The Boy had the audacity to sound sincere. I could feel his earnestness. Strange.

"No need to worry for me, son. I'll see things are done right by the rabbits."

"I'm not talking about the rabbits. I'm talking about you, sir. What will you do? How will you escape?"

"I'm a Magician, Boy."

The Boy glanced toward the window, his eyes searching the darkness. But they didn't latch onto me.

Not yet.

It was time to build that burrow on the other side of the castle.

Chapter Three

Burrows are cozy places, though a little lonely.

They weren't always that way.

Once, all four of us lived in a burrow together, small puffs of fluff! The Magician had made a home for us in a drawer at first, with odd bits of fabric around the edges to keep us warm. But soon he decided that we needed to understand how to live outside of the castle. We were never to be treated as pets or property. We were rabbits.

As rabbits, we needed to learn what that meant. The Magician read us stories so we could learn how to be rabbits, for there were no real rabbits on the island. He read *Peter Rabbit*, which always made me very angry. Why should Flopsy, Mopsy, and Cotton-tail get blackberries for dinner and not Peter? Peter did all of the adventuring, and all he got was punishment. Perhaps that was the Magician's message . . . but

I don't think so. He just wanted us to be careful in the garden and in the forest. There's no Mr. McGregor on our island. But out there, in the rest of the world, one couldn't be too cautious.

Actually, there was a part of the island less safe than the rest. A part of the island we were never allowed to go to, even when we were girls. I suppose it's one of the rules: *Never go across the stick bridge!* I can't tell you what's on the other side of the wild river that divides Hybrasil because I've never been. But the Magician is afraid of it, I think. He told us there would be no going back if we ever crossed the stick bridge. The bridge looked flimsy, and the trees that loomed on the other side, dark and bony.

There was also fog.

I can't remember when fog has ever looked cheerful. It's creepy. And I can't think of any reason why I would attempt to cross the stick bridge.

As for my big sisters, Caragh, Isolde, and Rory, they weren't the kind of rabbits to disobey an order from the Magician, so there was no need to worry about them crossing to the forbidden side. True, they were strong spirited. Mum would have been so proud of them. But they were content to forage for food, dig burrows, and listen to the books the Magician read to us.

The Magician read *Watership Down* to us because I think he just really liked it. So did we. We especially enjoyed how he made all the characters' voices. (Though we were quite terrified that we might be related to the Black Rabbit of Inlé, which is kind of a grim reaper in the rabbit world.) The Magician assured us otherwise. We didn't realize that it hadn't even been written yet. The date on the inside of the book was 1972, some thirty years in the future! How could such a book even exist? Impossible! But what is more impossible, I ask you: reading a book that has yet to be thought of or becoming a rabbit (if you are not one already)? That was part of the magic of Hybrasil.

Our island was a place of strange enchantment.

People lived on Hybrasil, long ago, back before it disappeared the first time. They abandoned it, though, jumping in their boats as the Sea swallowed their beloved island. They left ruins just about everywhere. Lots of castle-ish structures and swirls carved into rocks. Henges and the remains of elaborate ornamental gardens strewn across the meadows. Why, if you look at any map from the 1300s, you'll see Hybrasil—a roundish isle with a cleft across the middle (that's where the stick bridge connects the two sides). It is really, truly there.

But then Hybrasil vanished from the maps.

I know this because I saw several such maps in the Magician's library. Books and secret journals, too. (I'm very grateful I could read before becoming a rabbit, because I don't know if a rabbit can learn to read.)

I guess Hybrasil didn't taste very good, for eventually, the Sea spat it back out again. Not as grand as it was before, but still magical. Who would want to face such an unstable fate, not knowing when the island might be reclaimed by the Sea? Only the bravest of the brave returned to Hybrasil.

The first was the Magician, back when he was young and courageous.

He took over the old castle, making it a special place for others who practiced magic. Only magical creatures could locate the island, for he placed it under a special type of enchantment.

Sometimes the island was there. And sometimes it wasn't.

We, however, didn't locate the island. We were sent here.

But we didn't know *any* of this at first, when we were still girls. We were just trying to heal our sadness. Then we became rabbits. Priorities change when you become a ball of fur. As rabbits, we just knew that we liked it when the Magician read to us from a rocking chair in front of his castle as we munched in the garden.

I missed my rabbit sisters. All gone off with the Boy on the boat. One at a time, off to find out where they belong.

And now it was my turn.

"You are going to have to hide better than that, Albie."

I froze.

I hadn't expected my burrow-in-progress to be found so quickly. I could've run, but why bother? Even if the Boy caught me, he couldn't take me from the island if I didn't want to go.

Better to pretend that I didn't care that he found me. Let him think I *planned* for him to catch me. That would make his mind spin like a whirligig!

"You know," he said, "we don't have to do it like this. If you come with me, you won't be sorry."

In case you're wondering, rabbits can roll their eyes. And I did.

"I've word of your sisters. I can tell you about them if you come out."

My sisters!

A cruel trick. Of course I wanted to know about them. Had they found each other on the mainland? What destinies did they choose?

"Wouldn't you like to know what happened to Caragh? The others?"

How dare he use them to bribe me! I huffed off as angrily as a rabbit could manage.

The truth was, I'd do anything to be with my sisters again. Anything.

Except get on that boat.

Chapter Four

Caragh was the oldest sister—she'd be fourteen now.
She was also the one who least liked being a rabbit. Not that
anything much pleased her. On some days, she was such a
moody creature, but on others, she would conquer the world
and lay it at your feet. Mum said to get used to it—that was
life with sisters.

Isolde, strange beastie that she was, would be thirteen. She
was also the most obnoxious person I knew, and I completely
looked up to her. Isolde feared few things and put up with very
little nonsense. I missed her keenly.

That would make Rory twelve, just a year older than me.
I hated when she left most of all. Rory was warm, fluffy, and
cuddly. The burrow was especially cold and lonely when she
finally took her place on the boat.

※ ※ ※

The whole boat thing started with Caragh. When the Boy first arrived, he had a long meeting with the Magician, which none of us were allowed to attend, or hear. (The Magician cast a spell on the room to keep all of the words in.) Then it was all decided.

"My dears," said the Magician as he walked out of the castle, leaning heavily on his cane. The Boy was behind him but then vanished down the path toward the beach.

"The island is sinking, so you must go. One at a time, for that is the rule." He saw me tapping my rabbit foot in annoyance. "What is it, Albie?"

Of course, he knew what my problem was but smiled at me sadly anyway.

"Alas, little one, my magic isn't strong enough to oversee a safe voyage for four rabbits at once. I'm an old man, after all. You will have to go one by one."

My sisters became quite agitated. The Magician waved his cane and said some words that none of us understood, which allowed us to speak. He did this occasionally—though the times between our conversations had grown longer and longer.

"I'm too old for this babyish nonsense," Caragh told the Magician, placing her forepaws on her haunches. Even as a puffy bunny, she could look more annoyed than anyone I knew. "Change me back right now!"

"It wasn't my spell," the Magician replied. "It's not my magic to undo. You know that, Caragh."

We had probably heard that a million times.

"You'll have to ride the ferry and follow the rules if you want to change back," the Magician said. "This was the best arrangement I could manage."

"What's the ferry? And what are the rules?"

"The ferry is the Boy's boat. And the rules, well—"

"Point me in the direction," she said. "I'll ride in that boat right now."

"But there's a price," said the Magician. "Magic always has a price."

Caragh didn't wait to hear the rules. She just scampered down the path toward the beach.

That was a year ago.

And that was the last I saw of her.

Chapter Five

I couldn't sleep, and not just because the burrow wasn't finished, with roots and twigs prickling my side. So many things were crowded into my little rabbit brain, it made my head hurt. The Boy would come soon and bug me to get in the boat, and the Magician would bug me to go with him. But what bugged me most of all was that the island was going to sink, and there wasn't anything I could do about it.

I thought of the many magical folk who once lived here. Those rare souls who found their way to Hybrasil and improved their magical skills tenfold under the tutelage of the Magician. Of all his students, the most powerful was Murien. She was more talented than anyone before her, even the Magician. It would have been normal to be jealous. However, if you are a true worker of magic, you don't feel jealous or envious of those who are more powerful than you are. You simply appreciate their gift.

The Magician sought to train Murien so that perhaps one day she would take over as caretaker of the island, for contrary to popular belief, Magicians are not immortal. There would come a day when the Magician would die. He hated the idea of no one protecting the island and letting it sink into the Sea again. At least that's what he wrote in his secret journals.

Yes, I read them. I am nosy by nature.

But Murien isn't on the island anymore. I couldn't tell you where she is, having only met her in the pages of the Magician's book.

And these days, I found myself wondering: *If the Magician can't stop the sinking, then who can? Is it even possible?*

Perhaps that sort of magic doesn't exist.

A soft breeze bringing the salty spray of the ocean danced across my whiskers, cooling the ache in my head.

And that's when I knew that maybe the only person who could tell me if the island really had to sink wasn't a *person* at all.

Swiftly I scampered out of my burrow and made my way to the Sea.

There's a connection between the ocean and all living things. Maybe it's because life needs water. I don't know, really. But people don't seem to understand the Sea the same way animals do.

Before I was a rabbit, I could see the ocean and hear the waves, and I liked them, of course. But I didn't hear the poetry of the Sea, the waves, the spray.

Gazing at the Sea always gave me time to think. Sometimes I dreamed there, even when I was awake. And when I listened well, the Sea herself spoke to me.

What does the Sea say, when she speaks? Just ask a sailor or a mermaid, and they'll tell you. The Sea speaks in poetry. Verses ride on her waves and melt into her foam.

This was what she said today:

> *"'Tis lonely and sweet*
> *On the island, on high*
> *And from a cliff watches*
> *The watcher.*
> *But there she will stay*
> *Not today to escape*
> *More twilights will greet*
> *The watcher."*

I supposed that I was the watcher, and she was saying that I'd stay on the island for another day or two. Excellent news. But that wasn't the question I'd come to ask.

I tried to find the right words, but as I looked down at the way the waves broke restlessly upon the rocks below, only small puffs of rabbit breath came out.

The Sea is a source of unending magic and has a temper, so it's best not to aggravate her. She can swallow islands whole.

That was what I came to find out. Was sinking the island something she *had* to do? Didn't she have a choice about it?

I glanced down at the violent froth below.

I didn't ask her.

I couldn't. Manners are important, and there just wasn't a polite way to bring it up. True, she shared her verses with me, but who was I, a rabbit, to question the Sea?

Fortunately, the Sea told me I had more time. Something I could definitely use. After I finished my burrow, I would go back and spy on the Magician.

And the Boy.

Clouds covered the moonrise like the cotton tail of a rabbit. I couldn't have asked for a more perfect twilight as I sneaked up to the castle. They were in the kitchen. Quick as a . . . well . . . rabbit, I jutted through a broken vent cover and ever so stealthily made my way to my listening perch.

"Albie has never listened. Not once do I remember her listening," said the Boy while picking at the plate of leftover colcannon. I could smell the cabbage and hear his fork pushing it around his plate.

"Not precisely true, lad. Albie has always been an exceptional listener."

Why, thank you, Magician.

"As a matter of fact, she is most likely listening to us right now."

Perceptive, Magician!

The Boy looked around, peering out the window, but it was much too dark to see me, even if I'd been there. Instead, I was above in the shadowy rafters, hiding behind a large beam.

"The trouble with Albie is what she does with what she hears. Never was there a more stubborn rabbit," said the Magician.

I'll take that as a compliment.

"I offered to tell her of her sisters," said the Boy. "Of Caragh. All of it. But she just hopped away."

"All of it?" said the Magician. "I wasn't aware there was an *all of it* to Caragh's story. Don't take me for a fool."

Ha! I knew it! Untrustworthy! The Magician wouldn't stand for such nonsense.

The conversation stopped. There was shuffling below. And pacing. It was the Boy's even and steady steps.

Oh, how I wish I could better see what was going on! But even the slightest move on my part might give myself away. Was the Boy shrugging? Was the Magician waving his cane maniacally at the Boy?

Then they continued. "We're supposed to be talking about Albie," the Boy said.

"Indeed. You'll need to work more quickly, more effectively," said the Magician. "She must make it off in time."

"So you have an idea, sir, of how much time we have left?"

"It's more of a feeling. Not a good one. Albie should have the same chance as the others."

But I don't want to go. Not yet.

"And you've told her of the mainland?" asked the Magician.

"I tried, but—"

"A poor job you did of it, then. There are many things to love on the mainland."

The silence seeped into my fur. I could almost feel a sigh coming from the Magician.

The Sea would have called that sigh wistful. She uses such words.

The Sea would have said that the Magician loves something on the mainland very, very much.

Or someone.

It was getting more awkward. I was deciding if I ought to

shuffle a bit to make them aware that I was right overhead, but then the howling began.

The howling came from the other side of the stick bridge.

"Aaaaaaaaaaaaooooooooooooowwwwwwww."

I didn't know what made that sound. The Magician might have, but we didn't talk about it.

It was an eerie sound, the kind that begs for locked doors and latched windows.

"Aaaaaaaaaaaaoooooooooooooooowwwwww."

The kind of sound that shakes bones and teeth and makes fur and whiskers stand on end.

I couldn't help shaking a little.

"AAAAAAAAAAOOOOOOOOOOWWWWWWWW!"

A sound that maybe could sink an island.

Oh, I know, creepy sounds don't make enchanted islands sink, but the more the Magician talked, the louder and more frequent the Howler became.

I missed my sisters so, so much at times like this. I think loneliness is the feeling of not having anyone to snuggle with.

There was only me and whatever was howling.

I'd pass on the Howler.

Chapter Six

"The Boy thinks you're being difficult," the Magician said to me in the garden before dawn. I was by the lettuces. Three types of lettuces!

I stuck my nose deep in the red leaves, which were my favorite, and kept my back to him. His remark didn't deserve a response.

"I think you're just being . . . you," he said.

There was a knowingness to his voice. He was trying to tell me something without actually saying it. That was the Magician's way.

"However, Albie, there's the issue of you leaving the island."

I started chewing vigorously.

"I cannot force you, but, Albie, *you must go.*"

I stopped chewing.

"Every day that you remain here creates more danger for

your departure. I'll not have you hurt, little one. Life out there is better than being here. There are many, many options for you."

I stayed put but turned my ears a smidge to hear him better.

"Albie, you have to go."

I snapped my ears forward again.

No, actually, I don't.

The Magician sighed. "Stubbornness will get you nowhere," he said.

When I looked up again, he was gone.

I went to the shore, to hear what the Sea might say, if she was in a talking mood. (And if I was in a brave, question-asking mood.) That's the thing about the ocean; she is always there. One hundred percent of the time. I needed to find a way to ask her about the island. But I'd let her talk first. It was only polite.

It was a whisper, a wind over waves and spray.

"Albie," she said.

> *"Albie, little fur queen,*
> *With ears aflutter*
> *And lucky feet.*
> *So many questions,*
> *In so small a form.*

Eyes overflowing,
Never knowing."

Well, she knew I had questions. That was something. Then she went on.

"Trust," said the ocean.

> *"Trust is placing your heart*
> *Inside of a box*
> *Even when you*
> *Yourself*
> *Do not*
> *Have a key.*
> *Trust is that moment*
> *Of finding the key,*
> *Opening the box,*
> *And giving*
> *It all*
> *Away."*

I didn't like the sound of that, I can tell you. Why was she talking about trust and boxes and giving things away? The only person I didn't trust was the Boy, and I'd never give him anything I couldn't get back again. Not that I had anything— the only thing that I actually owned was . . . me.

"Trust," she said again.

I think I got the point with the first poem, but the Sea is never one to stop when she gets going. And it is very rude to interrupt a poem. I might have done many naughty things in my day, but I have never interrupted a poem.

> *"Trust is the*
> *Beak*
> *Of a tiny bird*
> *Pecking through*
> *The glassy shell,*
> *Not knowing*
> *What lurks*
> *On the other side."*

I liked this one better. And she was right. Trust was about not knowing. And sometimes not knowing was good for a rabbit. And a person, too. For instance, not knowing what is on the other side of the stick bridge is probably a good thing.

"Trust," continued the Sea,

> *"Trust is planting a cabbage seed*
> *In the spring*
> *To shelter a rabbit*
> *In the summer."*

So she knew I'd been hiding and spying in the cabbages. Well, there's not much the Sea doesn't know.

But she won't tell all of her secrets.

She'll give you some poetry, and if you can't figure them out, too bad for you.

And right now, it was too bad for me.

I took a breath and pulled all the courage I could manage from the bottoms of my rabbit feet all the way up through me. "About Hybrasil—" I began.

> *"Albie, I found this in the depths of the blue.*
> *Your father would want it returned to you."*

And with the next wave, the tarnished medal for bravery that the prime minister of Great Britain awarded my papa washed up at my feet.

Chapter Seven

The last time I saw the blackened bronze cross medal, it was shiny and new. But September 1940 was a horrible time to be a child. And that's what I was back then, a little girl with three sisters and two parents.

And a war that changed everything.

I suppose if you were far away from the war, it might not be that bad. You'd have to give up some food and fabric for clothing the soldiers needed, but you'd sleep in your bed each night feeling fairly confident that you'd wake up again.

It didn't feel that way if you were a child in London.

We came to London from our home in Cork to help win the war. We loaded up, my mother, my father, and my sisters and me, and traveled right in the middle of the Blitz. Rory, Isolde, and I thought it was a grand adventure. But Caragh was old enough to know it was dangerous, and she was pretty grumpy about it.

When the bombers would come at night, Caragh would cry and Rory would comfort her, brushing her brown curly hair until it shone like silk. It should have been the other way around, since Rory was younger, but Rory had that way about her. She mothered her dolls, the younger children in school. Even as a rabbit she was always asking if we had enough to eat and making sure our burrows were cozy.

As for Isolde, she was ready to fight, right there and then. She was a warrior. She'd sleep at night with a pot and spatula next to her, convinced she could use them as a sword and shield if necessary. She was always the last one down into the shelter, backing in so she could face any enemy.

I should have paid better attention to what was happening, but I was only nine. I spent my days trying to make a new slingshot. I'd left my best one, from Papa, back in Cork.

I don't remember much of the Blitz, being the youngest. At night in the shelter, we took turns telling stories to keep our minds from the booms that rocked the basement and sent bricks and rubble tumbling down around us. I didn't like loud things. I still don't.

Why would a family take their small children to a war zone?

For two reasons.

The first was that my father was a pilot. He was one of only ten Irish pilots who came to help the Battle of Britain. He said that if we didn't aid our allies, it would be worse for the world, and that meant worse for Ireland, too.

That's the kind of person Papa was. Always thinking about what was best.

He flew a lot of missions, most heroically. They say that only the lucky ones survived to the end without being shot down. My father was unlucky. We lost him that November.

The second reason we went to London was that my mother was needed, too. You see, she was good with magic. Really good. And if you think that the prime minister of Great Britain was above trying magic to win the war, you are wrong. If it would save his country, he would have tried just about anything.

The prime minister had heard of my mum. Don't ask me how; that isn't part of this story. When the prime minster of Britain asks you to come over from your little house in Cork and try to save all of England (even though sometimes England wasn't that nice to Ireland; we were taught in school not to talk about it in polite company), you go.

And we all came with her.

In case you think magic can keep someone from dying during the Blitz, well . . .

It can't. We lost Mum only a few days after Christmas, the same year we lost Papa.

She helped as best as she could before she died. And she was smart and thoughtful. She had arranged a safe place for us to go if anything happened.

Hybrasil.

She knew where it was, of course, because she was magical. She must not have been there herself, because I don't think she'd have chosen Hybrasil if she knew that only the old Magician lived there, or that everything was in ruins. It wasn't the kind of place to send four young girls.

Why couldn't we go back to Cork? Why couldn't we go back to when everyone was alive and happy and living in our cottage?

I loved our home in Cork.

We called it a cottage, but it was a biggish house with two stories, fairly grand as far as Cork went. Caragh once told me we had a big house because Mum inherited it from a relative. She never said who. But honestly, who cared as long as it wasn't haunted by some old granny's ghost?

From the front, the house was white and proper looking.

Four windows across the top, all with lace curtains peeping out. Across the bottom half were two windows and a big red door that stood a good two feet above my father's head, and Papa was a tall man.

But the back of the house was not proper at all. There were ancient vines growing up the side, nearly covering it. It looked like a gigantic faerie house, the kind I made in the summers from branches and leaves and left out in the woods with a piece of cake as an offering. In Cork, if you didn't leave an offering for the faeries, they'd tangle your hair and sour your breakfast every day. Or so the legends went.

We all wanted to go back to the house in Cork. Caragh was in charge because she was the oldest. Unfortunately, when she was out gathering supplies for our journey, she let it slip to some grown-ups that we were alone. A lady from the Orphan Removal Society showed up at our flat in London soon after. She was a miserable creature named Miss Bronagh, with gray hair and an even grayer personality. Her tiny blackbird eyes flashed violet when she glared, which was a lot.

"No, girls, you simply cannot stay here without a parent. You're too young. It's not safe; therefore, it's not allowed." A small smile played on Miss Bronagh's lips. She was enjoying disappointing us. She didn't seem to give a fig about our loss.

"We understand," said Caragh. "We know we can't stay,

so we're making other plans. We've a home back in Cork." She sounded so mature.

"A house in Cork? You've a house in Cork? There will be no going back to Cork. That would be . . . far too dangerous," squawked Bronagh the Orphan Lady, like some sort of awful bird.

"Then where are we supposed to go?" asked Caragh.

Bronagh the Orphan Lady's eyes glinted in a hideous way.

I wished I had my slingshot.

"Your father is gone, and your mother perished in the Blitz. I've done my research. Your mother made arrangements, such as they are. I'm charged with following her last wishes. I'm not saying she was in her right mind when she made them, but nonetheless—"

I kicked her. Hard, right in the shin. How dare she question Mum's mind, or anything else about her?

"You're an angry one, aren't you, little sister?" she whispered through gritted teeth, not flinching a bit. Then she dramatically doubled over and grabbed her shin, crying out pitifully.

Rory approached the hag. "We are ever so sorry, ma'am. We've been through a hard time. Please forgive our sister."

The hag continued to rub her shin pitifully.

"What if we won't go? Because WE WON'T GO!" I shouted, priming my foot for another kick. Isolde and Caragh held me back.

With Rory's help, Bronagh rose slowly. Caragh and Isolde released their grip on me, and I huffed off.

The hag limped over and put her face right in my face. She whispered so that her words were only for me.

"Of course you'll go, you stupid little girl. You think you can just do anything you want? You've got a lot to learn about the world."

I'll never forget her violet glare.

Then she straightened up, adjusted her coat, and smiled at Rory, Isolde, and Caragh, as if the whole kicking thing had never happened.

"Come, my dears," she said. "You've not much time to pack. Grab your things."

Bronagh the Orphan Lady had booked our journey, handing Caragh a sealed brown envelope for whoever met us at our destination. The boat was creaky and old, with hideous ancient-looking birds that trailed in its wake, dive-bombing us from time to time as if in battle.

Where we were sailing, we didn't know. Luckily, the Sea gave us easy passage.

I can't remember how long we sailed. None of us could. Most of the time we spent crying gently in each other's arms, mirroring the light rain from the soft clouds overhead. Then one morning, sunlight burst through the gray. There, where nothing was but a moment before, sat Hybrasil, glimmering before us like a broken jewel upon the sapphire sea.

Caragh delivered the brown envelope to the solitary inhabitant of the island.

I'd never seen a more shocked look on anyone's face.

I didn't give the Magician an easy time of it. It wasn't his fault that we'd washed up on his doorstep, on his island that was supposed to be hidden and that nobody was supposed to be able to find. Our mum was good with directions, I guess. Or more likely, good with spells, even spells cast before her death.

Those first days on Hybrasil were the worst of my life. And I made certain that everyone, *especially* the Magician, knew it. If there were a contest between the Magician and me to see who was the most horrible in our early days on Hybrasil, it would have been a draw. He was surely terrible and grumpy. His clothes were crumpled, and he smelled stale and dusty.

He didn't hug us or welcome us, really. He looked confused mostly, muttering unintelligibly and puttering off in the opposite direction. We were on our own a lot in the beginning. Caragh decided who would sleep in which room in the castle and made sure we were fed. Rory kept track of us, which was the hardest job, since that meant keeping Isolde and me out of trouble. Isolde was everywhere at once. She loved the freedom of the island. She found every hiding place and staged pretend battles.

I, on the other hand, was only interested in making everyone feel as miserable as I did.

Didn't anyone else care that our mother and father were gone?

I didn't understand the way they played house on this stupid island, like it was just some kind of adventure and not the worst thing that ever happened to us.

I don't think even the Sea would have understood, but we weren't speaking to each other yet, so I don't know. I blamed the Magician for our situation. I put grubs in his teapot. I put gravel in his bed and soaked his socks in cabbage stew.

He was worse, though.

He didn't even learn our names, or even try to. He just called each of us "girl."

Sometimes I'd catch him crying. I never thought to ask him why.

If only I would have talked with him when I thought of my stupid plan. If only he'd reached out to me, or any of us, before it was too late.

But even on an enchanted, hidden island, a person doesn't get do-overs.

Chapter Eight

You might be wondering why I'm not eager to leave. I've not painted a very friendly portrait of the island or the Magician. Why wouldn't I be rushing onto that boat?

Simple, really.

On Hybrasil, I knew what to expect.

In life, when something bad happens, there are people who say things couldn't possibly get worse. That's what I thought when Papa died.

Then the war took Mum, too.

Not knowing what was happening in the world made me want to stay on Hybrasil all the more. Besides, how was I supposed to trust the Boy when all he did was take my sisters away?

Speaking of the Boy, I hadn't seen him all day, which was strange. I'd expected him to hound me, nag me, beg me to get in that boat. I'd been practicing my not-listening-to-you stance. But there was no sign of him in the garden, in the hills, or by the Sea.

That meant he was probably in the castle, which was where I wanted to go.

Well, he could nag all he wanted. I wasn't afraid of him. If I wanted to go to the castle, that's what I would do. His pestering was like a little flea. Not enough to change my mind.

So to the castle I went.

"If you've come for stories, Albie, they're not mine to tell." The Magician was in his library alone, which was strewn with dozens of open books. He was calmly drinking tea, which meant that he was working, not just reading.

It was impolite to interrupt his work, but I had reasons.

The Howler wasn't as loud tonight, but I could hear it.

"Aaaaaaaaooooooooooowwwwwww."

I closed my eyes, buried my head in the armchair, and tried to ignore it. It got a little louder. I could feel it.

"Aaaaaaaaooooooowwwwwwwwwwwwwww."

I continued to pretend it wasn't there.

I jumped up to the table, landing on a book. The Magician put me on his shoulder so he could continue reading what looked like ingredients for a spell. Or a salad.

Carrots.

Radishes.

Cabbage.

All things he had in the garden.

"I will miss vegetables," he said. "I truly will."

I guessed he was talking about the island sinking, but I cocked my head and flicked my ear, trying to look like I didn't understand. Communicating with non-rabbits can be difficult. Rabbits understand all manner of subtlety that is completely lost on humans. I just wished that I could speak to the Magician with words, as he sometimes let us— but then I stopped myself mid-wish.

On Hybrasil you couldn't go around flinging wishes to the air and not expect some sort of consequence.

"Ah, Albie, what has become of all this?" Did he mean the library or the whole island? There was despair in his voice, like when we first arrived.

Then he gave me the gentlest smile. "Quite a pair, we are. Neither of us wanting to let go of things here."

He scooped me up, moved his pile of books to the side, and gently placed me back on the table. He scratched me between my ears, which is quite a wonderful feeling.

"Looks like I have a story for you after all, Albie. I suppose, at this point, it wouldn't be so bad to tell you a few things. Things I've kept secret for so long."

I looked around for the Boy, to see if he was skulking about.

"I've sent him on an errand. What I'm about to say is for your ears only. You'll have to decide later if you want to tell him, or anyone else."

Then he sighed one of those big sighs, just like before a wave breaks, loud yet breathy at the same time.

"I'm tired of being the keeper of secrets." He reached over, grabbed his cane, and waved it over me once. He mumbled something, but even with my superior ears, I couldn't make it out.

"There, now we can actually talk for a while," he said.

"Okay, that's what I thought we were doing," but instead of just thinking it, I said it. "Ah, so that is your plan, for us to talk to each other?"

"Don't you think it's about time?" he said. Then he went on, "You know the island is sinking, of course."

"And you're trying to save it, right? That's what you're doing with your spell books and your tea."

"Can't be done, I'm afraid. My magic is too weak."

"But is the . . ." I didn't have the word here. I'd always

thought of it as *the Howler*, but I never talked about it with anyone. Not ever. But since I could still hear it, faintly in the night, I supposed it was a good time to ask something that had been bugging me. "Is the Howler making the island sink? It if is, maybe if we destroy it, then—"

"No, Albie. I'm not even sure what a *Howler* is."

"You can't hear it?"

"I don't have rabbit ears. But sometimes things just sink into the ocean because they should and their time is done."

"Or," I said, "maybe they sink because they give up, which is really kind of horrible. Shouldn't you never give up?"

"Maturity is knowing when to give up," the Magician said. "And then it is called letting go."

"You can call it whatever you want, but it's still giving up. Still cowardly." To be a coward was the most awful thing in the world.

The Magician shook his head sadly.

"No. Sometimes letting go is courageous."

"I doubt that," I said. That was the sort of thing that cowards told themselves so they wouldn't feel bad.

Bravery meant not giving up the fight. It meant doing what was needed, just like Mum and Papa.

"My, you are an argumentative rabbit. Do you want to hear my tale or not?"

I nodded.

"Well, then, I suppose you've read of Murien?" he began.

I wanted to say no because if I said yes, then he would know I'd been snooping.

When I didn't answer, he went on.

"She was better with magic. I was simply a magician. She was . . . different. While I could control and use magic, she *was* magic."

He let the words sink in.

"But of course, I couldn't control her. No true magician can control another, nor should that be the goal.

"I would love to tell you what she looked like, but I can't find the words anymore. Sometimes, though, I can see her as clearly as if she was standing right in front of me."

The Magician reached out his hand as if to touch an invisible cheek.

"But of course she isn't. And yes, Albie, I did love her very much."

I hadn't even asked, but when a person reaches out to touch an imaginary face, it becomes pretty clear.

"The short of it is that we were married. The long of it was that the union wasn't as happy as we had both hoped. When she left, she was with child, but she never told me. Never told me about our daughter.

"We disagreed about magic, if you must know, Albie. I could tell you were about to ask but thought better of it. True, it would have been bad manners to ask, which is why I saved you the trouble."

The Magician—always one step ahead. Except he was going on and on. I tried not to yawn (talk about bad manners), but my whiskers started twitching fiercely.

"I thought we should share some of the magic we had developed with the rest of the world. She disagreed. She thought the world had its chance with magic long ago. The world prefers science. You've seen it yourself, Albie. You know it is true."

I knew nothing of the sort. I was distracted by something else the Magician had said. Something that started forming a thought in my sleepy brain until *snick*, there it was, snapped into place. *Never told me about our daughter.*

I was the most awake I'd ever been.

"She took our daughter when she left. But our daughter was of land and sea and magic. Children who are born of magic retain some of it. But of course you know that, Albie. You know it well. So Murien, talented Murien, took our daughter away, before she was born. I would have mourned if I had known about her at all. I would have liked to have met her—my daughter. She was of course also *your mother.* I heard from her only once. A ripped shred of a note."

He pulled a crumpled brown envelope from his pocket and took out a yellowed piece of torn paper:

I am sending my children into your care. Look after them.
Your daughter

I recognized the swirls of her handwriting, and my eyes filled with tears. I remembered exactly the way she would curve the end of the *A* when she wrote my name.

I reached up to touch the note. My eyes rested on the words *Your daughter.*

"Sometimes I wonder, if she knew about me, why didn't she ever come?" he whispered.

"Murien was my mother's mother. She was my . . . *grandmother*," I said at last.

The Magician nodded.

"And that would make you my—"

"Grandfather."

He was looking straight at me, into my black rabbit eyes, expecting . . . I don't know what. Maybe that I'd jump into his lap and let him hold me. (I was tempted.) I had always wanted a grandfather.

But I stayed where I was and whispered, "When were you planning to tell us?"

"I wasn't," he said. "If Murien had wanted me to know

about our daughter, she would have told me herself. She never did. She must have thought I wouldn't be a good influence on any of you. And the truth is that I'm an old hermit living out his days on a sinking island. I've nothing to offer the world. Nothing to offer granddaughters. She must not have wanted me involved at all."

I twitched a little. The same twitch I do when something sad makes me cry. But it was only a small twitch. Don't think that I was feeling sorry for him.

"So why now?"

His face looked older and more wrinkled and tired than I'd ever seen it, like if you took a piece of paper and wadded it up a thousand times, then flattened it out, then wadded it a thousand more.

"Why not now?" he asked. "There's very little I can do to you that you haven't already done yourself. You are a curious rabbit, more curious than any cat I've ever known, that is for certain."

His voice was tinged with pride.

"You've only a few minutes of talking left, Albie, until the spell fades. I apologize for the poor state of my spells these days. No matter how hard I try, I'm just not the magician I used to be."

He shook his head.

I said, "None of us are what we used to be, if you think about it."

This made him laugh. I don't think the Magician did that very much these days, for he wheezed like the hinge on an old door.

But it was good to see him laugh.

"You're right. You're a rabbit who used to be a girl. I am a wash-up who used to be . . . somebody."

We had a quiet moment.

I wanted to find a question (I had so many!) that didn't sound terrible or petulant or ridiculous. But instead, I found myself asking the one that had been on my tongue for months. Maybe years.

"What's going to happen to us?"

"The island will sink to the bottom of the sea. I'll sink as well. It is as it should be."

Just as I thought, but hearing him say it was horrible.

"So that is your plan? You really intend to let Hybrasil sink and go down with it?"

He sighed. "I've tried everything. Sometimes you can't fight fate."

He scooped me up again and held me. "And it's not your fate to remain here. You and I both know it. You must leave, Albie. Now."

Chapter Nine

I needed a plan. I couldn't let the Magician, my grandfather, sink into the ocean. I went to my usual spot, but the Sea was in no mood for poetry. I listened for her words, a bit of verse, perhaps a rhyme or two, but she just crashed into the rocks below.

What was wrong with her?

Probably nothing. Some days were like that. She had ocean worlds to watch over and didn't need to be bothered by a rabbit with a problem.

Still, I stayed. Sometimes when you are lonely, just being near a friend is enough. You don't need their words or anything they might be able to give. You just need to know that you're not alone.

That is one of the best feelings.

So I stayed with the Sea while she threw a tantrum against

the rocks. I understood those well enough. I knew what it was like to be angry about things you can't change. If my sisters had seen an ocean tantrum, they might have understood mine a little better.

Eventually, the foam became fluffy and creamy, fading back into blue a little slower than usual.

"No poems today?" I said, trying to sound jokey and light.

> *"I do not feel like poetry today.*
> *There is only water in my veins*
> *And today the water*
> *Is cold."*

Well, that was a little poetic.

"My words are soulless."

A bit extreme.

"You tell me a poem, Albie."

I was no poet. However, speaking with the Sea was different. There was a certain loveliness and connection, no matter what was said.

And so I tried a poem:

> *"Swish, swoosh,*
> *The wind blows over the top of your waves*
> *Exploding into tiny spray babies that find their way*
> *Across my rabbit nose.*
> *Diamond dewdrops linger on my whiskers."*

Her response was quick and surprising.

> *"Lovely, my pet.*
> *We'll make a poet of you yet."*

It was nice trading verses with the Sea, but I knew she had more important things do to. The sun was beginning to set, and the yellow glimmers across the water danced rhythmically to the horizon.

Sometimes, when I'm thinking about one thing, I'll have a memory of something entirely different. This time, it was when my hair was shortish and brownish, parted on the side and held out of my face by a gold clip, just the color of the glimmers on the Sea.

There was a hairbrush in my hand, and I pulled hairs off it. We had only one hairbrush between us—one of the few things we packed during our quick exit to Hybrasil. I was sure I had at least one strand from each of my sisters.

That was what the spell required. At least one strand from each girl.

I shook my rabbit head. I didn't want to remember what I'd done and was surprised to feel drops of dew scatter from my whiskers. The Sea had been busy while I pondered.

The Sea was always busy.

"Why does the island have to sink?" I asked her boldly.

"Why do bees buzz?
Why do peaches have fuzz?"

"Not all islands sink," I said.

"What do you know about the world, little one?
How many millions of years have you kept the counsel of
the Earth and her secrets?

I am guessing the answer would be none.
If the Earth wills the island to sink, then that is what
will happen.
The will of a rabbit is nothing compared with the will of
the Earth, even if the former is very stubborn and very
adorable."

At least she had given up the rhyming.
"Isn't it magic that makes the island sink?"

"What is magic, Albie?"

"That's what I've been trying to figure out."

"When you have the answer, you will have all the
answers."

I promise I didn't roll my eyes.

"Some things cannot be changed,
but that does not mean the ending is preordained."

Before I could ask the Sea another question, like why don't
you just say what you mean, she sent a wave made almost
purely of foam that whispered:

"There is a place you've been before,
There you'll find magic, and truth, perhaps more."

I knew the place, all right, but I didn't know that the Sea knew I'd been there.

It was forbidden.

If I did go back, I didn't know what I was supposed to do there.

There was a howl on the wind, and it gave me a chill, but a bird or two flew across the sky and gave me hope.

Sometimes hope is a dangerous thing.

Chapter Ten

It was stupid to go to the other side of the stick bridge.

I knew it, and I did it anyway. But I had to before I left Hybrasil. Leaving seemed inevitable—my choices were shrinking—leave or end up sinking. (Now I was rhyming! Spending too much time with the Sea.)

But first, I had to check every possibility.

As if pulled by an invisible rope, I made my way to the edge of the stick bridge and prepared myself to cross.

The first stick broke with the touch of my paw. The river below thrashed ominously.

This was more dangerous than I remembered.

I tried again. Better. If I was slow and careful and willed myself to be light, I just might make it.

I have no idea how I made it across the first time, back when I was a girl. I know I said I'd never gone, but I lied.

I clambered over like a chimp, no doubt, because the Magician said, "Never go."

I'd just lost my parents, for goodness' sake. I wasn't about to listen to some old man.

And now I was going again.

When I'd gone before, we hadn't been on Hybrasil long. The Magician hadn't been prepared for our visit and had no idea how to care for children. He let us run wild.

I was the wildest. My knees were forever skinned, my hair a mess, my skirts ripped.

There was no Howler back then.

I let myself dream for a minute that if I put everything back, just the way it should be, then I could save the island.

It was a lovely dream, hopeless perhaps, but it was the only one I had.

I stepped off the bridge.

All was still, no breeze. Quiet. It was daytime. The Howler mostly cried at night, when it was dark.

I was tempted to call out *"Hellooooo."*

But I was too scared. Maybe it was quiet here on purpose, so I could do what I was supposed to do and then vanish back across the bridge as fast as a wink.

I was quick, jumping from one place to the next, over tree stumps and large, exposed roots. I skittered under fallen logs without breaking my stride. I'd be there soon, if everything was still the way I remembered it.

Before, I had just wanted to get away. I'd stolen books from the Magician and wanted to see what I might be able to do. But I knew nothing of magic. Our mother, who was quite accomplished, felt we shouldn't learn magic yet, we were too young. Just because she was a magician didn't mean that her children should run around casting spells and such. If she had been a doctor, would her children be expected to perform surgery? If she'd been a lawyer, would they be prosecuting criminals? Absolutely not. Magic was a job just like being a physician.

It was not for children.

Magic just didn't seem that special to us. We never used it at home. We had no more idea of what our mother did when she performed magic than of how our father managed to fly a plane.

But on Hybrasil, I thought maybe I could do a spell to bring her back. I had to try.

The Magician's books were hard to understand. I was a pretty good reader, but magic books are filled with all sorts of unusual nonsense words that sound like someone wrote down the sounds a person made when they gargled.

What I understood from the spell that was called *Reditum*

Vitae was that if I did everything correctly, I could return my mother to life, and then she could help me do the same for my father.

But I had a little problem with the words *hair* and *hare*.

✳ ✳ ✳

Down a narrow path, on the far side of the island, there's a shack made of stone with a holey thatched roof.

I had gone into the shack and put the spell book I had stolen on the table. No one would think to look for me there, and I'd have the time I needed to perform the magic.

How hard could it be?

I pulled out the four hairs from my pocket. (There were other things, too, but those are secret. We can't have children everywhere transforming people.)

As soon as I said the last word, I turned all four of us into rabbits.

Becoming a rabbit felt odd: smooshy and soft. I suppose it could have been much worse. And if you're thinking that I didn't try to change us back, you're wrong. I tried everything I knew, which wasn't much. I searched that stupid book over and over again, but turning pages in secret are hard with only paws and a nose.

Clearly, I failed.

The howling started that very day and continued into the night.

My spell had made something here very angry. I didn't think about it at the time, but it wasn't too long after that the Boy showed up and started meeting with the Magician. Eventually, the Magician talked with us about our destinies, the Boy's boat, and the sinking island. Now things clicked together in my brain, making perfect sense: *I* made something on Hybrasil angry enough to *sink it.*

Maybe I could do something to make it happy so it would stop howling and stop sinking the island. While I couldn't return the magic, maybe I could trade with the Howler—something else *really* special for the magic I took without asking. Something the Sea had given me only recently—a hero's medal from the prime minister.

I rubbed it once more for luck. It had gotten me back across the stick bridge, and though I didn't want to give it up, it was time to let it go and make the trade. I slipped the medal's ribbon from my around my paw and let it fall onto the same table where I had cast the spell two years ago. It should have been a small sound, but an ominous clank echoed throughout the room.

"Hellooooo!" I called, cocking my head from side to side. I wasn't surprised that I had an actual voice here, for things across the stick bridge were always different indeed. "It's me, Albie. I'm the one who cast a spell. Anyway, I'd like to give you something to replace the magic I stole. I didn't mean to steal it."

There was a slight whooshing sound. It might have been the start of a howl.

"I've got this for you. It was my father's, but you can have it."

The wind rustled, a whistle-y noise. I shivered as the sound deepened, slowly and lyrically turning into a song.

It was a tune my father used to whistle, back when we lived in Cork in the overgrown cottage.

The whistling got closer, and the door of the small shack creaked as it opened.

"Well, hello, my little bunny," a voice said.

A man in an RAF uniform scooped me up and held me against his chest.

"I have missed you so much," my father said softly into my fur.

Chapter Eleven

No, magic can't bring people back once they die. I knew this to be true. Yet, here I was, sitting on my father's lap, on the forbidden side of Hybrasil.

Somehow I'd conjured something I wasn't supposed to. Again.

His hand stroked my back and stilled my quivering. I melted into it.

"How are you a rabbit, Albie?" he said. "It is you, I know it is."

It was a long story, and one I was sure we didn't have time for.

"How is it that you are . . . here?" I finally asked. It didn't seem to surprise him one bit that the rabbit he held spoke back to him. That should have been my first warning.

"I was out on a training flight. Had a bit of trouble with the engine, so I put her down here."

He motioned to the medal on the table. "That's a fancy thing. Where'd you get it?"

"It's yours. You wanted to keep it in a box because you said it was showy to wear a medal, but Mum liked it pinned to your uniform. Remember? 'For protection,' she'd say."

She'd probably cast a spell on it or something. A lot of good it did. Sometimes bullets and bombs are stronger than magic.

"I only just learned to fly, Albie. You know that. How would I have earned a hero's medal?" he said, looking wistfully at the medal, then out the window at the sky.

I stared at his profile. His nose was the same, but his hair was a little longer than I remembered, and there were no little gray hairs like there were the last time I saw him. He was thinner, too.

"Papa?" Even though I knew it was him, it had to be, at the same time, he just wasn't the same. He seemed much . . . younger.

Perhaps . . . *it hadn't happened?* The shooting-down part. Not yet.

My mind was spinning. From what the Boy told me of his boat, and of the island itself, *maybe Hybrasil had moved to a time where my father was still alive.*

And if so, was there even the slightest chance that I'd get to keep him?

He hadn't stopped petting my back and between my ears. He didn't seem to mind at all that I was a rabbit, which should have warned me for the second time. But I was too happy; there was no room in my brain for rational thoughts. (To be fair, a rabbit brain is a little smaller than a human brain, so there is that.)

"Are you . . . Oh, Albie, this is ridiculously hard to ask. Are you a dream?"

"Well, no, I'm not a dream. And maybe you aren't, either."

He didn't say anything.

"You're here because this island, well, it moves around," I continued.

"Islands don't usually move around, love."

"This one does. It moves *through time.* Do you understand? The island probably moved to a time before you got—" I covered my mouth with my paw.

He thought for a moment, trying to puzzle it out.

"I'm dreaming that you're a rabbit and that I'm having a conversation with you about disappearing islands," he said, chuckling.

Maybe it was *my* dream, except that I was certain I wasn't asleep. No, I was here, on the far side of the island across the stick bridge, and my father was holding me.

I wanted this moment to last forever.

But my stupid curious mouth asked, "Where is your plane?"

He carried me half on his shoulder like I was a baby. We went out of the crumbling shack, through a dark forest, and into a clearing where his plane sat, bullet-free and very much intact.

"It's here. Are your sisters here, too? And are they . . . rabbits?"

He wasn't at all concerned. And that was when I knew he didn't believe any of this.

And if he didn't believe it, he'd never stay.

"Yes, Papa, they're rabbits. But they left. And it was all my fault."

"How can the fact that I have dreamed you as a rabbit possibly be your fault?"

"Because it's not a dream!" I said forcefully, as much to myself as to Papa.

He laughed, a deep laugh that I used to love. But I didn't think it was funny, so I bit him. Not hard. But enough to get him to drop me. Then I hightailed it into the forest for a good think.

Papa just stood there shaking his head. I saw him pinch himself on the hand, probably to see if he felt it. If it was real.

How could I convince him? The Magician probably could, but there was no way he'd come across the stick bridge, even if I begged. Even if he knew who was on the other side.

※ ※ ※

It was getting dark. Maybe it was the clouds blocking the sun, or maybe the sun was going down earlier than I expected. I wasn't the master of time, since rabbits rarely wear watches (except for the White Rabbit in *Alice in Wonderland*).

As for the Howler, silence.

For the first time since . . . well, for the first time *ever*, I found myself wishing the Boy was here. For some reason, I thought he might have an idea how to handle this, but I didn't think he was the kind of person to cross a forbidden stick bridge.

But maybe it was time for him to break some rules.

Chapter Twelve

I found the Boy in the Magician's garden, pulling up carrots and radishes. He gathered his vegetables and walked toward the castle, looking behind him at times to see if I was following. I was, stealthily.

The Magician met him at the door, balancing shakily on his cane.

"Any progress?" asked the Magician.

The Boy shook his head.

"You're a persuasive boy. You'll think of something."

The Boy regarded the Magician closely. "If you'll pardon my saying, sir, you look . . . unwell."

"The outward is often a reflection of the inner. Always remember that," he said, tapping the Boy gently on his shoulder with his cane. "Now come and sit. Standing makes me tired."

They sat in the parlor. On silent paws, I followed, close to the wall. There was dark-stained wainscoting, and I was gray as a shadow, so I blended in rather nicely. The parlor was arranged with couches and daft-looking chairs.

I never spent much time in the parlor. Now, having scampered behind a velvet settee, I could see there were some important things that I hadn't noticed before.

The woman in the large painting above the fireplace was smiling at me. The truth bloomed in my heart, she looked a bit like Mum but with different hair.

It had to be Murien.

Then something shifted. If I'd looked away for a second, I would have missed it. The blue of her eyes rolled like waves, swirling into an image of my mother, then me.

In her eyes was . . . the Sea.

The Sea was my grandmother.

How in the world had Murien become the Sea? That was magic I couldn't begin to understand, but deep inside, I knew it had to be true. If a girl could become a rabbit, then maybe a woman could become the sea. Perhaps it wasn't that different after all.

But I didn't know what to do with this knowledge. I would think about the ocean tomorrow. Today I needed to figure out how to save Papa from getting shot down from the sky.

The Magician and the Boy blathered on and on about insignificant things—when radishes lose their sweetness and become peppery hot. I hoped the Magician would go to sleep soon so I could talk to the Boy. I'd have to point to letters in books so the Boy could write them down and string together words and sentences (since I couldn't talk to him), and that would take a long time. I was getting restless in my spot on the bottom shelf of the bookcase, squeezed between a few old encyclopedias and a truly hideous vase.

"Listening in again, are you, Albie?"

Drat. The Magician always knows when I'm near.

"There's not enough time for games anymore, little one. There's conversations to be had. Come along out now." Not a request. A command.

As I revealed my location, I knocked the vase a little with my tail.

"I knew you were there," the Boy said.

Sure you did.

The Magician waved his cane over my head and said, "I suppose there are a few things you need to discuss." Then he left me and the Boy alone.

"So he made it so you can speak?" said the Boy. "Isn't really fair, since that's one of the perks of the boat. Rabbits can speak on the boat. Makes the boat seem less special."

"Follow me. I can't talk to you here," I said, liking the sound of my voice now that I really listened to it. Voices are wonderful things. Ever so useful. Some people don't appreciate them. When they don't speak up when they need to, bad things happen.

"Come," I said.

The stick bridge was creepy in the daytime. I could only imagine how terrifying it would be at night. But now, right before dusk, when the shadows were at their longest, the stick bridge looked like the skeleton of a giant snake.

Maybe this wasn't a great idea.

But the Magician was right: we didn't have time to dawdle.

"I have a proposal," I said.

"Well," the Boy laughed. "This is a first. None of your sisters thought to marry me."

I snorted in disgust.

"Not marriage, dolt. More of a bargain. You give me something, I'll give you something."

"There is only one thing I want, Albie—for my job to be done. And in order to have that, you'll have to—"

"Yes. I know. And I'm willing." My voice shook a little. Voices are also betrayers.

"You'll come with me, on the boat, and discover your destiny?"

His eyes were alight. He really, really wanted this.

Made me wonder why, but instead of asking, I nodded. Then: "The condition is that you have to come across the stick bridge with me."

He looked over at it. Now that the sun had almost completely set, it didn't look so menacing.

"I don't think it will hold me."

"It's stronger than it looks." *And so am I.*

He pondered the bridge. "And what do we do when we get to the other side?"

It didn't sound like he knew it was forbidden, which was probably a good thing.

I said, "I need to show you something. And I need your help."

"Why?"

"I need to stop the island from sinking. There's magic there, on the other side of that bridge. Big magic."

"Big magic or not, it can't be done."

"Then I won't go with you."

He hemmed and hawed and paced. But he knew that few things are as stubborn as a rabbit.

"This is a bad idea. The Magician forbids anyone to cross."

"It's not that bad. There's something you need to see. Don't you want to save the island? And the Magician, too?" I made my way over to the bridge and put a paw on its creaky steps. I could feel the coarse spray of the wild river below against my fur. Not the gentle spray of the Sea at all.

"I do want to save them, Albie. Believe me. But first I have to get you safely to your destiny. So even if we come up with a plan, we have to wait to implement it until you're safe."

Implement. *Such a fancy word for a boy who rows a boat.*

"You're putting your chickens before the horse—or something like that. Let's just cross the bridge and see, shall we?" I said. And I slowly started across the bridge.

He waited until I was all the way over before he stepped on it. He said if the bridge went down because he was too heavy (he was a string bean of a boy, so I hardly thought it likely), he didn't want me to get hurt.

If the bridge wanted him to cross, I was certain he'd be allowed over. If not . . .

"I guess this is stronger than it looks" was all he said as he jumped off my side. "Now where to?"

I led the way past the woods to the clearing where I'd first seen my father's plane. It wasn't there.

"Papa!" I called out. "Where are you?" I scampered this way and that, searching for him. I sniffed the air, hoping to find his scent.

The air was cool and empty.

"*Papa!*"

"Albie, what in the world are you doing?" the Boy said, annoyed.

"I'm looking for something." *Someone, actually.* Under the light of the full moon, the wings of my father's plane would have gleamed impressively. There would be no missing it.

Except that it was truly gone.

That meant Papa was gone, too.

"Papa!" I cried once more, racing into the little shack.

"Your father? But he's—" The Boy trailed after me.

"Here. Papa was here," I said, jumping up on the table.

The Boy shook his head. "No, Albie. You must be mistaken."

"And his plane was here, too. He flew it."

"What? No, Albie, no. That would be . . . wrong," said the Boy.

"He *was* here." I stomped emphatically and threw my paws up in disgust. I knew what I'd seen.

The Boy sniffed the air. "Interesting."

He scratched his head. "Albie, maybe you were dreaming or had a memory or even a vision. Yes, a vision, perhaps. But he couldn't have been here, you know that. People don't come back from the dead."

"What makes you an expert on the living and the dead?" I asked him.

He was quiet, contemplating my question. "Nothing. I'm an expert on nothing," he said sadly.

"I conjured him here. I had his medal, and I was at the magic table . . ." But the medal was no longer there. "I didn't imagine it!" I leaped from the table and hopped out again to where Papa's plane had sat.

The Boy followed me outside to the vacant meadow and bent to give me a comforting rub. I bit his finger, just like I had my father's.

"Ouch!" Holding his finger, the Boy walked around the perimeter of where the plane had been. "I'm not saying you imagined it. I'm just saying that this is a very magical place, and all is not always what it seems."

And then it began.

"Aaaaaaaaaaaooooooowwwwwww."

The Howler was back.

"Albie, what in the world is that?" the Boy cried, placing his hands over his ears.

The Howler was much louder on this side of the island.

"It's a long story!" I tried to shout. But it's hard enough for a rabbit to be heard, even with a spell. He just looked at me kind of stupidly, trying to read my lips.

It's impossible to read a rabbit's lips.

We rushed back into that weird little shack and closed the door behind us. The howling didn't stop, but it was quieter inside.

"Seriously, Albie, what is that?"

Hm. How much to tell?

As if in answer, I felt the island sink a few inches beneath me. It was time for the truth.

I started out slowly, but then the sobs came and the words rushed out.

"I came here when I shouldn't have, long ago. I stole magic by turning my sisters into rabbits, even

though I didn't mean to. Then something magical got mad and started sinking the island. And howling. Terrible, terrible howling. All because of me. It's all related. Magically related."

Maybe I was speaking another language, because the look the Boy gave me said, *I didn't understand a word you said.*

"Think about it, if there's enough magic to bring my father here, then maybe there's enough magic to keep the island from sinking!" I was hopping up and down wildly, quickly getting out of breath.

He could believe or not, but I really wished he would believe.

He ran a hand through his hair, which made it stick up in a funny way, but I was too upset to laugh. "Perhaps your medal conjured a vision of your da because you love him so much. It's not an unheard-of phenomenon. But it wasn't him, not really. That could never happen. And, Albie, neither you nor your Howler are the reason this island is sinking."

"How do you know?" I cried.

"Two reasons. First of all, this island has sunk before. If you paid any attention to the legends about it, you'd know it to be true."

I wasn't stupid. I knew the legends. I was about to interrupt, but he continued before I could.

"That's what this place does. It submerges, then it reemerges. It has nothing to do with you."

"And the second reason?"

"The island isn't sinking because of you. It's sinking again because of me."

Chapter Thirteen

The Boy and I trudged back to the castle. I left a little part of my heart on the other side of the island with Papa, even though he maybe hadn't actually been there at all. Still, one way or another, I'd seen him again. That's a lot more than most people get when they lose someone they love.

I sighed like I was more ancient than even the Magician.

I felt a million years old.

Even though the Boy hadn't helped me save my father, or the island, I would hold up my end of our deal. The old me, back when I was an angry girl, would have broken her word to the Boy. But I was learning.

Broken words can do lots of damage.

I would get in the Boy's boat and sail across the Sea to the mainland, but I wouldn't abandon my task. I wasn't finished trying to cheat death and save the Magician. But unless I went with the Boy, he'd never tell me how Hybrasil sinking was his fault. Maybe the Boy's secret might help me save the island after all.

Until I knew for sure, I'd have to settle for saving the Magician. And I'd need a place to take him.

The Boy wasn't the only one with a secret.

There was also the Sea.

I had to tell her what I knew before we left.

I went alone to the beach.

> *"Farewell, adieu.*
> *Until the final sun sinks*
> *Until the last blade breaks*
> *Until the words that complete*
> *The ultimate story*
> *Dance across the ending page,*
> *I will be there.*
> *You are not alone."*

I don't know how she knew I was leaving, because I'd just decided, but she did.

I liked where this poem was going—because I *was* afraid.

"Thank you," I whispered. *"Grandmother."*

My voice was so quiet, I didn't even hear myself. Perhaps I hadn't said the word at all.

But I heard it, an echo murmuring upon the foam.

Grandmother. Grandmother. Grandmother.

But she didn't say anything to me. Maybe she didn't know what to say. Maybe it happened so long ago that she didn't remember being Murien or having a daughter or loving a Magician.

As unusual as it was, I had no words.

I had to say goodbye to the Magician. I couldn't have him thinking he would actually see me again. That was my secret, if everything worked out as I hoped.

On my last morning, I hopped across the garden to the dilapidated castle for the last time. The Boy was gathering vegetables for my journey.

"Ah, Albie. Come to say goodbye?" the Magician said.

He was sitting in the parlor again, curled forward in a large wingback chair.

I hopped over and tried to speak, but the spell had worn off.

"I shall miss you, Albie. I shall miss you most of all," he said, causing my eyes to fill and overflow. "Oh, how I loved your grandmother." His voice cracked. "However, while the ocean might decide to visit, she can never stay. And this is something I should have known."

It's hard to watch an old person cry. Actually, it's hard to watch anyone cry, except maybe for babies. They cry all the time. But for everyone else, it is like watching an egg crack and all the goo sliding out.

I wanted to tell him that I already knew Murien was the Sea. But sometimes there are things inside of you that you can't share, even though they are bursting to get out.

He scooped me into his lap. "I didn't think I would feel this sense of . . . of loss when you left. You're leaving an empty hole inside of me. You're the only one who knows I am your grandfather."

I leaned a little against him then. He was my grandpa, after all.

"But you are a good girl, and it's time for you to go." He picked me up and placed me gently on the floor. "I'm sorry I won't be able to see you choose your destiny and change back. But I can give you this." He tapped my head with his cane, his body visibly weakening as he cast the final spell between us. "Even off the Boy's boat, you'll always have your words now."

Thankful as I was to have been given a voice, I said nothing, because sometimes there just aren't any words. I was actually going, by my own choice, on the dreaded boat. Leaving everything behind, hoping that things wouldn't be worse wherever I ended up.

When it was time to go, the Magician carried me to the boat and placed me gently inside. It was the most tender thing I remember, ever in my whole life.

A white bird tried to perch on the side of the boat, but the Magician shooed it away. Instead, it flew above us as the Boy and I drifted away from the island of Hybrasil. I listened for the sound of the Howler, for surely it wouldn't let me leave without a final irritating wail to pierce through my courage.

But there was nothing.

The Magician watched from the beach as we disappeared

into the foam and mist. I wonder what he did, in that moment when he knew he was alone.

It was too sad to think about, so I chose to simply look at the white bird, flying in and out of the clouds, just as we floated up and down among the waves.

"So, Albie, where is it you want to go? The world awaits you—nearly any time or place—within reason, of course. No going backward in your own time, because, well, it's complicated. I mean, you can't go to a place you already are. Just remember. That's a no-no."

I could speak now, whenever I was ready, but I let the silence settle around us like a cloak, soft and ethereal.

The Boy was content with the quiet, too.

He rowed for quite some time.

When Hybrasil had disappeared into the mist for the final time, I turned to the Boy and said, "It's time to meet my destiny. Take me to the mainland. We've got sisters to find."

"What? No. Albie, that's quite unreasonable."

He paused. But I'd made my decision, and nothing he could say would change my mind.

"How about this," he said at last. "I'll tell you what it was like for each of them, each of your sisters. Maybe once you hear about each of their journeys, you'll realize that finding them is a poor excuse for a destiny. There is so much out in the world—so much more. You'll have no choice but to see the truth of it."

He was wrong about that.

But I did want to hear of my sisters. I twitched my nose in agreement.

"I'll start with Caragh." And so the Boy began.

Part II

In Which
I Search the World
for my Sisters

The Boy Speaks:
The Story of Caragh

When Caragh got on the boat, she wasn't afraid, not
a little. That was because she knew it was the right thing to do.
All rabbits need to get on the boat to go back into the world.
That's how it's done, Albie.

There's a lot of time to talk on the boat. Usually we get to
know each other well, the rabbits and I.

Caragh told me her favorite thing on the mainland was the
circus. She remembered all the interesting and unusual people
who traveled and performed. She thought they were so very
glamorous.

"I'd like to be in a circus, Boy," she'd said to me.

"Would you, now?" I said.

"Yes. I do love the circus."

There are many circuses on the mainland. Caragh wasn't

the only person who loved them. The trick was to find the one that was perfect for her. But she didn't quite understand this.

"Just a regular circus. And hurry up about it, Boy. I'm tired of being a rabbit," she said.

When we reached the shore, I borrowed a bicycle I found by the dock. We raced to find a circus. Remember, the rabbit stays a rabbit until she completely agrees with her placement in the world. Then she changes.

And then there is no going back—I'm certain about that.

Fairly certain, anyway.

Caragh rode in the bike basket, and I pedaled like a fury. Over hills, through villages, in and out of cities, looking for a circus.

"A circus has striped tents," Caragh said. "And sometimes elephants. Look for the elephants."

It didn't take long.

I walked up to the tent. "I'd like to talk to the ringmaster," I said to a small man in a stained shirt, with long hair and an uneven mustache.

"Why?" said the man.

"This rabbit wants to know what kind of circus this is."

"The rabbit wants to know?" said the man.

"Yessir. The rabbit wants to know."

"What rabbit?" said the man, looking at me strangely.

"Why, this rabbit, of course," I said, gesturing to the basket, but Caragh was gone. What I didn't know is that the enchantment upon you rabbits is quite remarkable, even more so on the mainland, where people don't much believe in magic anymore. Anyway, when Caragh got scared, she vanished. Completely invisible. I do wonder if that is a gift all of you rabbits possess. Can you do it, too, Albie?

(No, I can't. Caragh could make herself invisible? How?)

"Caragh?" I called. "Caragh? Where are you?"

I heard her scamper behind the edge of the tent. I went over and whispered, "Caragh, it's all right."

"I'm scared, Boy," she said.

The mustache man appeared and whispered over my shoulder, "Whatcha got there, lad?"

I wasn't skilled in the ways of diversion—not yet, anyway—so I told him.

That was a mistake.

"I've a rabbit, but you can't see her. She's scared."

"Wait a minute, lad! You've got a rabbit that really, truly turns invisible—a truly magical rabbit?"

"I—I—guess so," I replied. "Now, Caragh, come along. If you don't like this circus, I can find another one."

"You'll do no such thing, lad." His voice was in my ear, and I felt something poking me in the back. It was probably a knife. I didn't want to back up into it to check. I froze.

"Make the rabbit appear again, or it'll be your liver on a blade!"

(I gasped, and the Boy looked pleased.)

I stood very still, hoping she was still close by.

"Caragh, this man is going to stab me in the gut if you don't come out."

Caragh was a kind girl. A girl who knew the right thing to do. She appeared, and the man swooped her up by her rabbit ears and thrust her into a bag.

"Ooooh, such a pretty silver thing you are!"

"Now wait just a minute!" I cried. I couldn't imagine what the Magician would have done if he'd been there.

"Here ya go, lad. Here's some coin for yer troubles." He stuffed some sweaty coppers in my hand.

"No! This rabbit is *not* for sale!" I cried.

"I should say she's not. She's already sold!" The man laughed. "Going to make meself a fortune with a rabbit that is truly magic."

He grabbed a moth-eaten top hat and placed it jauntily atop his long, stringy hair.

No place for a rabbit, let alone one who was trying to change back into a girl.

The Ringmaster put his face close to the bag and spoke

roughly. "This is how it's going to be, rabbit. You will appear
and disappear when I say, or you will become a fine stew.
Understand?"

There was no sound from the bag. What could she say?

What had I done? My first job and I'd botched the whole
thing.

I couldn't leave her behind. The least I could do was to stay
with her. So, I got a job gathering hairs for the bearded lady.

Her name was Maxine.

"Why's a fancy young gent as yourself working for the
Ringmaster?" she said to me one day as I was dropping off that
day's collection, a few gray snippets, half a horse tail, and a
lovely blond ponytail belonging to an obnoxious girl who kept
yelling at the cat tamer, "Kill them all!"

"You come from money. I can see it on you," Maxine
continued.

"If you can see such things, then why don't you work as the
fortune-teller?"

"Ha! That's a crock, even worse than my fake beard. This
isn't even a proper circus."

I knew that now. I wish I had known it when I'd brought
Caragh here.

Caragh had two shows per day. One in the afternoon and
one in the evening. She dutifully hid in the Ringmaster's hat until

he pulled her out by her ears, then she vanished right before their eyes. The Ringmaster never let go of her.

After the show, the Ringmaster put her in a small cage. He kept the key on a chain around his neck all the time.

I had to find a way to get Caragh out of the mess I got her into, and get her to a proper circus. Unfortunately, word of the amazing magical rabbit had swept across the county. Folks were lining up to see the show. The Ringmaster was raking in the coins.

Caragh was more and more distraught.

One day, before I took the day's collection of hair to Maxine, I stole a moment to sneak over to see her in her cage. She looked thin and pale.

"We must find a way to get you out of here," I whispered.

She nodded.

Her fur hung like an ill-fitting coat. I had to do something soon, or there'd be nothing left of her. The Magician had told me my task wouldn't be easy. I should have listened better when we made the arrangement.

"We're getting you out of here, Caragh. Now. Today. You'll do one more show, and that will be all." I whispered my plan to her, watching for spies.

The Ringmaster stumbled in. "Get yerself away from my rabbit, Boy."

"Of course, sir."

"None of that *sir*. No putting on airs."

"Of course not, sir—I mean, I meant no harm."

He glanced over at Caragh, nearly skin and bones. "I need to fatten her up. She looks pitiful." Then he addressed Caragh. "I'll cut yer legs off for luck if you give me trouble."

He thrust a carrot in front of Caragh, who dutifully ate it, then he stuffed her in the hat for the evening show.

Folks filled the bleachers, and the line outside circled the tents twice. I could see the Ringmaster sizing up the crowd to see if he'd have enough to do another full show.

The circus began with the cat tamer. No, not a lion tamer like you might have heard of in other circuses. This was a smallish circus, so there were only smallish animals. Trained cats slinked across tightropes with no net below to catch them. Everyone knows that you can't really train a cat, anyway. Cats do what they want to do. The trick is to find a cat that wants to walk a tightrope.

There were no elephants or larger animals, unless you counted the baby llama that had somehow made its way from the other side of the world to the mainland. Sitting on the llama's back was a trained marmot, Felix. Now, Felix was a stubborn marmot who didn't like to do tricks, but the audience loved him all the same.

A few other acts came and went—some very sorry-looking clowns and some pipers who needed a good deal more practice.

"You, Boy!" the Ringmaster hissed in my ear. He pulled me by my arm and shoved me over to a rope ladder. "One of my trapeze artists is ill. The people want a show! Get up there!"

I had no idea about swinging from one rope to another, and I wasn't about to learn during a show, but the Ringmaster sneered and said, "If you don't, the rabbit won't live out the night."

I was wearing only regular clothes, but I guess it didn't matter. Valiere, the lead flier, pulled me onto the platform and handed me the bar. "It is easier than it looks, mate. Just swing a few times, back and forth, then Wals will toss you the other bar and you switch. Got it?"

"No."

"I'll make it easy for you. You let go of this bar and grab on to that bar, or you fall. Do you understand now?"

I gulped.

There was no net.

"Go," said Valiere.

"I'm not ready!"

"Go anyway," said Valiere, and shoved me off the platform.

I soared over the heads of the crowd, my legs kicking wildly. I'm sure I looked quite ridiculous. Then back again I went. Then forward.

"Pump! Pump your legs," cried Valiere.

I did as he said, hoping it would be enough to see me to the other side.

I decided maybe it didn't matter. If I fell, then that would be quite a distraction. And we needed a big distraction.

Of course, I might die or become crippled. Isn't it the Magician who says there's always a price for things? If the price for saving Caragh was my life, was I willing to pay it? Don't look so worried, Albie. Since I'm here, sitting next to you, obviously neither happened.

(I was not looking worried, though my tail may have been shaking. Blasted tail.)

Still kicking like a fool, I let go of the bar and reached with flailing hands for the one Wals had sent flying across to me.

Time stopped, or so it seemed. I'm sensitive to time. One couldn't sail the Sea around Hybrasil and not know how to navigate such things. I looked down at Caragh. She believed I could do this.

One sweaty palm grabbed the bar and started to slip. I flung my other hand, reaching from my toes to my fingertips until I got both hands on the bar. The roar of the crowd I expected to hear was more of a groan.

They were disappointed I hadn't fallen.

Wals reached out and pulled me up to the platform on the far side. "See, not so bad, eh?" I didn't answer. I just climbed down the rope ladder, shaking like a leaf in the wind.

Then it was Caragh's turn. The Ringmaster did his usual hammy act. He was so full of flourish, it oozed out of him like an overripe banana from a rotten black peel. He reached into his hat and grabbed Caragh, who appeared as we had planned. The crowd clapped, but not with much enthusiasm. They've all seen this trick before. Then the Ringmaster said some flibberty-jibberty words, and then Caragh, right on schedule, vanished into thin air.

Now the crowd was interested! This was what they had

come to see! Even better than a boy falling to his death.

Enter Maxine.

"What're you doing here?" roared the Ringmaster, dropping the invisible Caragh. "You're in the second half. Get yer beard outta here!"

"Do NOT yell at a lady," Maxine warned, her beard blowing in and out with her breath. "I am Maxine, the Bearded Lady!" she cried, addressing the audience. "What type of amazement have you wrought, Ringmaster?"

This was just the distraction we needed. As Maxine, who towered over the befuddled Ringmaster, asked him to pull something else from his hat, Caragh escaped.

I raced to the back of the tent, where we had arranged to meet. She stayed invisible, as planned, and I placed her gently in the basket of the bicycle that I'd stashed behind a tree.

I pedaled hard, till my breath burned against my chest and my lungs ached and wheezed.

When it was safe enough to stop, I did. I panted for a bit, then realized the sound I was hearing wasn't my own pitiful gasping, but Caragh.

She was crying. And there's not a more heartrending sound than that of a rabbit crying.

(I remembered that sound well. We all cried. At least at first.)

"Caragh, what is it? Why are you crying? We escaped. You'll never have to work for that horrible idiot again. I'll find you another circus, a proper one this time."

"I don't want a proper circus. I don't know what I want!" she cried.

I tried to reach out and soothe her, but then she turned invisible.

"You don't have to go to a circus at all. I'll take you wherever you want to go—whenever you want to go. You can go to the past, just not your own, or how about the future? It's yours to choose," I said.

So, that's the story, I guess.

Oh, you didn't expect that, did you? Well, neither did I. Caragh just vanished. Hopped away—still in rabbit form! I searched and searched for days, weeks, months on end.

You're wondering if I found her? Well, I didn't.

Chapter Fourteen

The Boy's story about Caragh made things harder than I thought. How would we find her when we didn't know where to start? Finding the circus where he'd left her seemed logical, but even though the Boy had been to this part of the mainland before, we were lost.

"I told you this was an awful idea. Besides, the thing about circuses is that they travel!" he muttered, carrying me and stumbling along the road leading to yet another town. He'd left his boat tied to an old dock that he thought looked familiar.

He might have been mistaken about that dock.

"You told the Magician that you checked in on my sisters. I heard you."

"I might have made things sound a bit more . . . favorable to my own situation than they were."

"Obviously."

The landscape was very green, but rocky as well, as if it couldn't decide what kind of place it wanted to be—inviting or foreboding. The foreboding part kept me from wanting to hop along on my own. And there was the fact that the Boy owed it to me to carry me around for a bit. It was a bumpy ride, but it could have been worse.

As if it read my mind, the wind blew a soft moan, just like the Howler when it starts up. *How did it get here? Had it followed me?* No, not possible. We were much too far away from Hybrasil to hear the actual Howler.

I flattened my ears to my cheeks so I couldn't hear the wind.

"I thought you could take your little boat wherever you wanted to," I said. "Can't you just tell it to take you to Caragh?"

"That's not how it works. I can navigate to a loose time frame, and of course, places are a little easier to find. But going to an exact place or time, or both, is something I'm afraid I'm rusty at."

"You can only be rusty at something you were once good at." Then, much more quietly, I said, "It doesn't seem like you were ever good at it."

He pursed his lips but stayed silent.

"How will we know when we are close?" I asked.

"We'll know. People will say something about a circus being near. They won't be able to help themselves."

And soon enough, the Boy was right. We found a circus.

This was far grander a circus than the one he told me about. As we got closer, my whiskers twitched. I could feel she was close.

The tent wasn't striped but a solid, magical shade of rich purple with white silk flags flowing in the wind. The Boy carried me inside his shirt, just in case there was another horrible ringmaster.

I supposed I should change into a girl. It might be easier to find Caragh if I could walk on my own. Not to mention, I didn't want to be threatened with a stew pot. I leaped from the Boy's arms to find someplace a little less public. I dashed behind some bushes and thought hard about changing into a girl, about who I was before. There really couldn't have been more to it than that, could there? The Boy had taken me to my destiny (finding my sister), and now I wanted to be a girl again. Easy peasy.

But something was wrong. I remained just me.

"Change your mind?" asked the Boy when I returned after a few minutes.

I nodded. No sense in worrying him.

"Just as well," he said.

No one looked familiar to the Boy. He kept looking for Maxine the Bearded Lady, but she wasn't there.

What if Caragh had been recaptured? What if something had happened to her while she was still a rabbit? What if she hadn't become human again?

In those few minutes, I felt a thousand kinds of awful. Caragh had never liked being a rabbit. Not at all. And it was all my fault.

I said little prayers under my breath, hoping she was okay.

We made our way to the tent, taking one of the few seats left high up in the risers. As the Boy was tucking me back inside his shirt, an amazingly tall woman made her way to the center of the ring.

"Maxine!" I gasped. She was just like I had pictured her, except beardless.

Maxine welcomed the crowd and bowed with a flourish, the tails of her coat flapping behind her.

The Boy raced down the bleacher steps, nearly slamming into Maxine as she stepped out of the ring.

She looked at the Boy and scolded, "Watch yourself, young man."

She looked at me and gasped. She cocked her head from one side to the other, her eyes never leaving me. "You look very familiar . . . but . . . no."

Slowly her gazed shifted to the Boy, and she gasped again.

The Boy bowed respectfully. "Pardon me. It has been a while since I was here. Things have changed."

"Indeed," said Maxine, a bit flustered. Then she regained herself and spread her arms wide. "Welcome to my circus."

She led us out of the tent and over to a large poster, pointing to it with her ringmaster's whip.

MADAME MAXINE'S CIRCUS: COME AND BE AMAZED!

FELIX THE MAGNIFICENT
WILL ASTOUND YOU!

FERNANDO THE LLAMA
WILL INSPIRE YOU!

THE FELINE AVIATION SOCIETY
WILL LIFT YOUR SPIRITS!

CARAGH THE GLORIOUS
WILL BLOW YOU AWAY!

Caragh the Glorious. She was here! My little rabbit heart thumped in my chest. The first stop on my journey to complete my mission was going to be successful. I puffed up a little. Maybe this wouldn't be so hard.

But what did she do that blew the audience away?

"So, the circus is yours now?" the Boy asked Maxine.

"This is a completely different circus altogether. I'm the ringmaster."

"But Felix, he was the marmot, right?" the Boy asked. "How is it that he's with you?"

Maxine chuckled. "Felix, Fernando, and the cats all came to me because I'm a better boss and I pay them well. Besides, it's more fun working for Maxine. Instead of trying to find the right circus, Caragh and I created one."

"She's here?" I said.

"This rabbit talks?" Maxine asked.

"You can hear her?" the Boy asked.

Maxine nodded.

"Is she Caragh's sister?" Maxine asked.

It was my turn to nod.

Maxine led us back into the tent. "I'm sure you want to see her, and you will, but first, she must do her two o'clock show."

Instead of sending us back up the bleachers, she led us to a fancy roped-off section that had seats with cushioned backs. "My private box seats. Enjoy. And, little one, you are safe here. No one will harm you."

I climbed out of the Boy's shirt and took the seat beside him. We watched as the marmot rode on the llama and as the cats swung on the trapeze—they had moved on from tightrope walking.

Then Madame Maxine went back to the center of the ring and called out, "Now we have come to what you have all been waiting for. Caragh the Human Cannonball!"

The crowd went wild, and I felt sick to my stomach.

Across the purple tent, I saw her. She was a girl again, tall and willowy, in sparkling silver sequins. Her hair was in golden brown waves around her head. Very grown-up. She sashayed from the tent opening to the enormous cannon that had been wheeled in by two gentlemen in tuxedoes. She was waving confidently, like she'd been shot out of a cannon a millions times.

Nervously I tapped the Boy. "We can't let her do this."

Annoyed, he whispered, "How can we stop her?"

"I could scamper out, create a commotion, you could grab her, and we run away." It wasn't my best plan, but I'd had worse.

"Albie, I can't do that."

"Why not?"

Madame Maxine had appeared next to the Boy with a box of popcorn. "Oh, you'll want some of this. It's my own secret recipe. Nothing makes you hungry for popcorn like watching some cannonballing."

Absently the Boy took a handful and stuffed it in his mouth.

"Albie, I can't because this is her choice, not mine. Remember what I said about choosing destiny? Caragh has chosen hers."

"It's DANGEROUS!" I said, causing several people to turn around. A talking rabbit was not something people expected to see, even at a circus. Flustered, the Boy placed the popcorn box in front of me, and I made myself small.

Madam Maxine recovered for him quickly. "Of course, this IS dangerous, young man! Only the brave Caragh can master the cannon."

Caragh was climbing up the side of the giant cannon now.

I couldn't let her do it.

I slunk down between the fancy box seats and the ground. The Boy hadn't noticed. But he would. I'd have to be fast. I raced through the crowd and across the giant ring. Caragh was at the top of the cannon, ready to lower herself in.

She saw me.

Her head tilted to one side.

Then the other.

She sniffed the air.

"Albie?"

I nodded.

She climbed down the side of the cannon. There were boos from the crowd, who obviously wanted to see her explode across the sky. "Albie," she said as she hugged me.

As best as I could, I hugged her back.

She scooped me up into her arms, then lifted me over her head.

The crowd cheered.

"Caragh! Put me down!" I squeaked.

But she just shook her head and started back up the ladder with me under her arm.

"Quit squirming, Albie. It'll be fun. And besides, you deserve this."

She was seriously going to shoot me out of the cannon with her!

"Caragh! No!"

But my rabbit voice wasn't nearly loud enough to be heard over the crowd. I looked to see if the Boy had any idea what was going on.

His head was turned to Maxine, and they were both examining a kernel of popcorn. They had no idea my life was about to end.

"Caragh! I came to stop you from this nonsense!"

"Oh, listen to you, wild little Albie. Being so protective! Do you realize how funny this is, you being the scared and nervous one?"

We were now at the top of the cannon. Caragh was climbing inside. I wanted to scream, but my scream would have been puny.

Once we were inside the cannon, Caragh did something strange.

She transformed into a rabbit!

"It takes much less explosive to shoot a rabbit across the tent. And then on the other side, I'll reappear. It's amazingly spectacular."

"No, Caragh! I'm supposed to be saving you. The Boy and I came from Hybrasil to save you!"

"The Boy is here?"

"*Ten . . . nine . . . eight . . . seven . . .*" Maxine led the countdown.

"What is she doing?" I cried.

"*Six . . . five . . . four . . .*"

"What do you think? Now hold on to me. And really, Albie, after all you put me through, you can consider this payback." She was holding me tightly with her rabbit paws, nearly squeezing me to death.

"Three . . . two . . . one!"

The sound of a cannon going off when you are inside is so loud, your teeth chatter. And then it's so loud that it's silent. But you don't even care because you're flying.

I've never flown before. My father never took us up in his plane because we were too little, and then he was at war.

There is nothing like flying. Nothing at all.

We zoomed across the tent, skimming the ropes and poles that held it in place. It felt like we were in the air a thousand years. Spinning, swirling, twirling. I was glad I hadn't eaten much before, because even though I was completely exhilarated, I was also a little sick to my stomach. And no one wants to be under a shower of regurgitated carrots.

I think people were oohing and aahing and cheering, but I couldn't hear it. My wonderful rabbit ears were completely nonfunctional.

Then we were falling.

And we were bouncing, up and down, in a big net, far behind the crowd. On the third bounce, Caragh was back to being Caragh again.

She walked over and lifted me into the air. The audience was on their feet.

I wanted to laugh and cry at the same time, which is probably what I did.

My big sister was holding me, and people were cheering.

My heart was lighter than I'd ever felt it.

Later, after the show, the Boy, Maxine, Caragh, and I sat around a small table in Maxine's tent. She had made vegetable stew and placed a bowl in front of me. I licked at it hungrily.

I was starting to think my plan would work. But to get it off the ground, I'd need my sister's support.

"Well, I have to say, Albie, you did great for your first show. Are you planning to stay with us, then?" Caragh's voice was tentative, like she wasn't sure what she wanted the answer to be.

"No," the Boy and I said at the same time.

He shrugged sheepishly. He knew this was my decision. Not his.

"You know," Caragh continued, between bites of stew, "if you changed into a girl, then a rabbit for the cannonball part, like I do, and then back to a girl, there would be no stopping us. We'd be the most famous cannonball sisters in the land."

"You're not supposed to be able to do that. It's not possible," said the Boy.

"What's not possible?" asked Caragh.

"Change back and forth, from a rabbit and back again to a girl."

"Well, it seems like you don't quite know everything, do you?" said Caragh sassily.

"I don't want to be a cannonball sister. It's not my destiny," I said, interrupting whatever was going on between my sister and the Boy.

She nodded, then tore off a chunk of bread, offering a bit to me as well, but I refused. Maxine and the Boy pretended that their stew bowls held the most amazingly wonderful things in the entire world. They were so polite, it was quite annoying.

"And what is your destiny, Albie?" Caragh asked.

The Boy's eating had slowed down considerably. He was interested in the answer, too.

"My destiny is to gather my sisters and go to our home in Cork. And I'm planning on bringing the Magician there before Hybrasil sinks."

Caragh was quiet.

The Boy choked on his stew.

"You could move your circus there," I said.

"Moving a whole life isn't that easy, Albie," Caragh cautioned. But she was thinking about it, I could tell.

"Perhaps Cork doesn't have a circus?" said Madame

Maxine, already warming to the idea. "I've always heard wonderful things about Cork."

"I'm not sure if the whole circus can actually move to Cork," the Boy whispered to me. "It might be difficult to manage. We'd have to use the boat and make many trips."

"We'll cross that bridge when we come to it," I said, hating the fact that I'd used the word *bridge*, because it made me think of the stick bridge and every mistake I'd ever made.

And the Howler.

I listened for it again. Nothing. Maybe I'd imagined that it followed me here.

Caragh still seemed a little hesitant.

"It's the Magician," she said. "I can't believe he'd want to come and live with us. Don't you remember how unpleasant he was when we first got there? It wasn't until we turned into rabbits that he gave us the time of day. Maybe it's best if he just—"

"If he just what?" I asked. "Sinks with the island? No. No one gets left behind. I know he was a cranky old man when we came. But he changed. When we became rabbits and you all started to leave, he changed."

I didn't say that the Magician was family. The only family we had left.

Families should stay together.

Caragh would understand. But I wouldn't tell her the truth in front of the Boy. It would have to wait.

"Very well, Albie. This is your destiny. You get to decide. The Boy will take us both wherever you want to go."

That was easy. Maybe too easy.

But then I noticed the way the Boy hadn't taken his eyes off Caragh—not really, anyway—and she didn't seem to have trouble looking at him.

And I realized that the only one who saw trouble was me.

Chapter Fifteen

Caragh and the Boy walked and I hopped to the Boy's boat at the dock.

"I don't understand why we have to get on the boat. We can go overland to Cork," Caragh said.

I decided to let the Boy answer.

"Uh, the boat is special. We can actually travel faster," he said, trying to sound important.

"The boat seems bigger than I remember. Stronger." But she was looking at the Boy when she said these things.

I thought the cannonball had made me nauseous, but watching Caragh and the Boy flirt was about all my stomach would take.

As we cast off into the Sea, with the Boy rowing and Caragh watching him with a stupid look on her face, I couldn't help but feel that this had been too easy. I asked Caragh to come with me and she came.

Would I be as lucky with my other sisters?

It started to rain.

The Boy had bought Caragh a scarf from a street vendor to cover her hair. It was navy blue, embroidered around the edges with lovely silver flowers. I didn't think the Boy should be buying gifts for Caragh. And Caragh shouldn't be accepting gifts.

Caragh scooped me up and snuggled me, sort of like I was her pet, but I didn't want to be a pet. I wanted to be her sister, her human sister.

But every time I tried to change, nothing happened.

There was the time behind the bushes. I'd tried again behind the scarf maker's stall. Perhaps I wasn't doing it right. But I'd chosen my destiny, what was the holdup?

I thought about talking to the Sea. Back when she was Murien, she knew a lot about magic. But she didn't seem the same here as she had in the waters by Hybrasil. She felt warmer, but distant. It was almost as if she wasn't there.

"Where to?" said the Boy, interrupting my thoughts.

"We're not going to Cork, not yet, anyway," I said. "We have to get Isolde."

Caragh's face lit up in a smile just as the Boy's darkened into a frown.

"Albie, this isn't a good idea," began the Boy. He saw me starting to protest and said, "Since you're going to ask why, I'll tell you."

The Boy Speaks:
The Story of Isolde

*Isolde wanted to go to a place that most people think
isn't real.*

She hopped into my boat and began talking right away.

"I want to go to a place that I dream about every day, but
there's nothing like it in history books. Rather like Hybrasil, but
different."

"You're going to have to tell me a little more than that," I said.

Isolde was young and brash and daring. To be honest, I was
afraid she would choose unwisely. The Magician said it wasn't
my place to advise, though, so I listened, if a little leery.

"I want to go where airships fly across the sky."

"Are you talking about *Peter Pan*? That's just a story. I can't
take you into a storybook, Isolde. You know the rules."

She got angry. And you know what happens when a rabbit
gets angry. Lots of thumping and kicking.

"No. I do NOT mean *Peter Pan*. I KNOW it's just a story. Where I want to go is like London but DIFFERENT. Like London but BACKWARD."

Isolde wouldn't consider another choice.

I shouldn't even be telling you this, but I'm not the only one who travels the Sea in special ways. There are others who are far more knowledgeable than I. They know where the portals are. Please don't ask me about the portals because I really don't know too much. I can only say that when you enter one, it takes you to the same place but *different*, where one little change creates a whole other world. Up until Isolde got on my boat, I had only heard legends of portals. But somehow Isolde knew there was one that would lead her to a London with flying airships.

I have to admit, it sounded like an exciting place to go, but I'd need a map to get us there.

So, we anchored off the coast and waited until dark, silently rowing back to Hybrasil. You've been to the Magician's Library, I think. If so, you know that he doesn't organize things in any sort of order that would make sense to anyone but him. However, I didn't want to ask him for it. It was my job to get the rabbits to their destinies.

Isolde told me that she'd know what book to find by the way her dream smelled. I've never smelled things from a dream, but then, I've never been a rabbit. She sniffed and sniffed until she found it. She pulled the book out with her paw. Then she nibbled the map page right out of the book!

She was a thinker, that Isolde.

And so it was that we set off, to a place that we'd been before, but not.

I won't tell you how we found the portal, or about the horrible beasts that guard it and that we had to trick.

You would just get scared, and my job isn't to scare you.

But once we made it past the horrible beasts, we arrived near England. We floated on the river Thames into London.

And sure enough, there were boats with propellers floating across the sky. No, not like the ones your da flew. Those were planes. These were different altogether. Imagine something like Captain Hook's ship, big and proper, with sails, but also enormous round globes and propellers keeping them aloft.

To fit in, I decided to get a propeller and flying sail for my small boat. I was terribly curious, was there magic afoot or machinery? Science or spells? Sometimes it's hard to tell the difference.

We traveled through the city as discreetly as we could until we found a shop called Shipley Goodes. It seemed like the perfect place to find what we needed.

Isolde hid in my satchel. I didn't latch it, so she could look out from time to time, except there wasn't much to see. I bought a propeller and a giant envelope of white silk that I was assured would transform my little boat into a miniature airship.

I walked giddily to the door with my purchases. The whole idea of flying my ship above the clouds was intoxicating. I had sailed every sea on Earth, but the skies were foreign to me.

I had a ridiculous grin on my face as I opened the door.

"Oh, a first-timer," said the young woman brushing past me as she entered the store. "Never flown before?"

"How could you tell?"

"You've got moons for eyes, and your hand is grasping that bag so hard— *Is there a rabbit in that satchel?*"

My face burned and my forehead started to sweat as I fumbled to cover Isolde. I don't know why I felt I had to keep Isolde a secret. It's not like they had a law against rabbits. No place had a law against rabbits. And yet, I didn't want anyone to know about Isolde until she had changed.

"Uh . . . ," I said.

"It *is* a rabbit!" she said. "Are you making rabbit stew for dinner?" She reached into my satchel and pulled Isolde out by the ears.

I reached for Isolde. "No!"

"Ah, it's a pet," said the young woman.

"No. She's nobody's pet," I said before I had the sense to think about what I was saying. Why hadn't I just kept my mouth closed and gone about my business?

"Maybe you're her pet, then," she said, handing Isolde back.

It was then that I got a good look at the young woman. She had chin-length brown hair that curled a little but not too much. And she had freckles and long lashes.

I hadn't really thought about girls being beautiful before then. And I didn't fall in love with her or anything.

(Caragh's nose twitched. If I hadn't been a rabbit, I wouldn't have noticed.)

There was just something about her.

"Come with me. I'll show you and your rabbit how to rig all this to your boat."

Without a better idea, I followed.

Isolde and I walked several paces behind her through the crowded streets of the place that looked like London but wasn't. She had long legs and it was hard to keep up.

"You could change now if you wanted," I whispered. "She's not looking."

Isolde seemed to consider the situation, then shook her head.

✳ ✳ ✳

The young woman's name was Janie Trafalgar. She was fourteen, almost fifteen. Practically grown up. She lived with her grandmother in a four-story house in the middle of a square. It wasn't a famous square, but even if it had been, you wouldn't have heard of it because it wasn't London, not really.

"Lulu," Janie said when we walked in the door. "We have company. It's a boy with a rabbit."

"I don't want rabbit for dinner," replied an elderly voice from upstairs.

"It's not for dinner, Lulu, it's his . . . friend."

Janie's house had a big table right where you walked in. "You can put your bag there. We'll see what kind of propeller you bought. And where's your boat?" she asked.

"Thames," I said.

"Oh. Well, we can get it in a bit."

Isolde was tired of being ignored. And tired of being a rabbit, too. She hopped out of my satchel and scampered into a corner, behind an old barrel, which seemed strangely out of place in this modern home. And there were clockwork bits mounted everywhere—as if everything ran on gears. None of it was shiny metal, but old brass and copper and lots of wood. All of it burnished.

In the time it takes to sneeze, Isolde had changed into a girl, catching me completely off guard.

She walked over to Janie and sniffed the air around her. I guess it smelled like her dream, because she let out a sigh of relief.

Janie turned around, and I gasped.

It was as if Isolde was Janie's long lost younger sister. And I wondered for a minute if it were possible. Same hair, same freckles, same lashes. Except that Isolde was a couple of years younger than Janie.

"Where'd you come from?" asked Janie.

"I'm with him," said Isolde, pointing to me.

Janie shrugged. "Oh well, then. On to flying ships."

Neither Janie nor Isolde noticed their resemblance.

However, Lulu, Janie's grandmother, came down the stairway and gaped at the two girls examining my newly purchased propeller. Lulu might have looked delicate, like a small gray moth that had seen better days, but she was still solid.

"Merciful heavens," she said, clutching her heart.

Both girls turned and looked at Lulu at the exact same time, wearing the exact same expression.

It was disconcerting to say the least.

"Where's your rabbit? Where did it go?" asked Janie.

"Uh—" I said.

"What rabbit?" said Isolde.

❋ ❋ ❋

The trick to getting a boat like mine to fly was in the engraved brass plate.

After you attached the propeller (which Isolde and Janie did after we had lugged my boat to the roof of their house by means of a clockwork donkey, a large wagon, and some sort of magic pulley) and you fastened the air envelope (which Isolde and Janie did also), it was time to think about the boat's name. This name gets engraved into a brass plate (by some device which must contain magic of sorts), and then the boat can fly. I guess the man at the shop thought I already had one—most boats got their names when they were christened for their first voyage.

I wasn't even alive for my boat's first voyage, for I'm not the first Ferryman.

It's an old, old boat.

"We have to give it a boy's name," said Isolde.

"You mean a girl's name, right?" I said.

Lulu, who was dishing up a nice stew for our dinner, looked up. "You are from London."

It was not a question.

"This is Nodnol, not London. Boats are named for boys here in Nodnol. And the ships are captained by women. Well, mostly, anyway," she said. "We get visitors from London on occasion. Those who've somehow slipped through. A nasty lot, most of them. Oh, sorry lad, I didn't mean to offend."

Yes, the place was called Nodnol. *London* spelled backward!

Isolde, her mouth full of brown bread, smiled so big that crumbs fell out the sides of her mouth and onto the table.

Everything seemed the opposite of things as we knew it.

And it was exactly where Isolde wanted to be.

If girls were captains of ships, she told me, they had to be warriors as well. She could almost feel the armor, heavy, but not overly much. And the sword.

(Isolde had wanted a sword, or a weapon of sorts, since that night in the Blitz.)

Isolde was ready to fight back.

"So," Isolde said as she wiped her mouth with the back of her hand. "What do you think we should name the ship? I think we should name it after a boy we both know." She didn't blink once as she spoke to me.

The only boy we both knew was me.

You are probably wondering now why I've never told you my name. There are those who believe that if they know your name, they can control you—that's why names often aren't spoken until the christening, when babies were protected with holy water.

Now, I'm not sure if I believe that, but I can tell you that names do have power.

And a smart person never gives away their power.

Remember that, Albie. If you remember nothing else I've told you, remember not to give your power away freely.

(He was so earnest in this moment, looking at me and not making eyes at Caragh. I nodded.)

"Bob?" I said with a bit of merriment I didn't feel.

"You are not a Bob," said Isolde.

True.

Isolde had finished her stew, and Janie gathered up her bowl.

"Nathaniel," Janie said. "Are you a Nathaniel?"

I thought about it for a moment. I wasn't a Nathaniel, but maybe I could pass for a Nate. I tried it out in my brain. Yes, I liked Nate.

"Not Nathaniel, Nate actually. Good guess."

Isolde snorted. She knew I wasn't Nate but had the grace not to say anything.

"All right, we'll get this engraved with *Nate* and then your ship will be ready." Janie was beaming. She liked being helpful. Janie and Lulu let us stay with them that night. They didn't ask questions about what we were doing in Nodnol without any family to visit or a plan for finding a place to stay. They were used to unusual visitors.

Isolde and I had rooms across from each other. I could hear her pacing on the other side of her door.

I knocked.

"I knew it was you. I can't sleep. I don't remember how to sleep as a person," she said, her silvery coat glimmering slightly in the starlight that streamed through her window.

"Well, you're going to have to try."

And it didn't matter much that she couldn't sleep because in a moment the street below erupted into a festival of shouting.

In half a second, Isolde was a girl again.

"What's going on?" we called as we raced down the stairs.

Janie and Lulu were already down there. Janie stood in front of a cabinet filled with weapons. She stuffed a sword in a scabbard at her waist and a small knife in her boot. She looked up at us, tossing us each a small sword.

"I suggest you wear these, if you know what's good for you. I hope you know how to use them."

My sword clattered to the floor at my feet, but Isolde caught hers swiftly and had it stuffed in her belt before I'd even bent to pick mine up.

"I've been practicing, *Nate*," she said with a smile.

First of all, how in the world would a rabbit be able to practice with a sword?

(*Would the Boy never learn what remarkable creatures we were? A rabbit could learn whatever she put her mind to.*)

"What's going on?" I asked Janie as she raced through the house, bolting all of the windows shut. Lulu was unlocking some sort of cupboard with a very tiny key.

"Don't douse the light yet, Janie. Let me get the pistols first!"

Pistols!

"Isolde, you are not to touch a pistol! Not at all," I said. "What would the Magician say?"

That thought kept racing through my head, round and round, dizzying me like a top. I was making a mess of things. Why had I let Isolde choose the portal? I know it wasn't my choice to make, but the Magician would've found a way to talk her out of it.

I was a failure.

But of course, this story isn't about me. It is about Isolde, who was choosing a pistol.

"What in heaven's name are you doing?" I yelled, grabbing it away.

Gently Lulu took it from me and handed it back to Isolde. "Not like the guns in London," she said. "This is Nodnol, remember? These pistols shoot magic—curses, if you will. Not bullets."

"Isolde doesn't know any magic," I said.

"And your rabbit just vanished, did it?" Janie raised her eyebrow smugly.

"It wasn't her doing," I said. And I couldn't say more than that, because that was the truth. Isolde hadn't cast the spell; therefore, it wasn't hers to undo.

"Shhhh. They're coming," Janie said when the house was

completely dark and there were no sounds inside the house or outside. I had never heard such silence before, nor have I since.

"You can take your chances and stay here," Lulu whispered. "Or you can come with us."

Isolde was already climbing the staircase, which led to a hatch in the ceiling to get to the roof and our airships. "I've been waiting to do this for a long time."

"I'll come!" I was the last up the stairs.

"What about my boat?" I whispered fiercely. "It's not ready to fly yet?"

Janie waved me on as Isolde squeezed past into the night above us.

"We don't have an engraver for your name on the brass plate, so we'll just have to wing it."

Janie grabbed the plate from me and flipped it over in her hands a few times.

Meanwhile, there was a clambering on the roof.

"My crew is getting my ship ready to sail. Isolde will be fine up there for a minute," Janie said in answer to my unspoken question.

"You'll need to cry," Janie said. "We don't have an engraver, so we'll use your tears. Can you cry on your own, or do you need me to hurt you a little?"

"What?" I asked, but before I'd even gotten to the *t* on the word *what,* Janie had reached into the edge of my nostril and yanked out a nose hair.

"Yeesh!" And then I actually cried a little. I would dare anyone to have a nose hair yanked out and not cry a bit. It's impossible.

"It's the fastest way," Janie said by way of apology. Then she put the brass plate near my cheeks and caught the two tears. There were only two, by the way.

She handed me the plate and we continued up the stairs to the roof hatch. "You'll need to trace a name on here, a magical name, and somehow I don't think Nate's going to cut it. Use your real name. Magic will know if you're lying. So, don't lie. Trace your name on the plate, and then place it on the bottom of the boat once we get outside. It doesn't matter where. If the magic works, the plate will stick there by itself. If it sticks, then you fly. If you lie, then . . ." She shrugged and cracked open the hatch.

"Lulu can't handle it by herself. And your little friend probably doesn't have much experience."

My tears were drying quickly, so I had to work fast. I traced my name, my real name, onto the brass plate, then placed it on the hull of my boat (which was still upside down, having just had the propeller attached).

The brass gleamed, then the boat swayed and rose in the

air, righted itself, and paused in front of me. A small mast and sails materialized, and a ladder rolled down the side of the ship toward me. I climbed up.

"Release your sails, and the envelope, too!" Janie called from the bridge of her impressive airship. It was ten times the size of mine, with sails taller than a castle tower.

Isolde leaned over the edge of Janie's ship, a sword in one hand and a pistol in the other.

"Get back!" I called.

But maybe she didn't hear me, for she leaned over the bow of Janie's ship. I was underneath it and to the left and could see its name, *Sweet Leroy*.

What kind of name was that for a ship?

The moon was big and golden, the type of moon you see only once a season, if that often. Against it flew the shadows of many airships, out to battle with . . . with what?

What were we about to battle?

I should have thought of it earlier, of course. Just as the Germans couldn't resist bombing London to attempt to win the war, so the pirates couldn't resist an attack on Nodnol on this night of . . . whenever.

Yes, we were being set upon by pirates. I know you're thinking about Peter Pan's ship. It's hard not to. But these pirate ships weren't shiny and clean. You could see the barnacles, kelp, and sea moss clinging to the hulls, shadowed eerily in the moonlight. These ships looked haunted.

I for one did not want to be captured by these pirates.

Their sails were black, making them seem like skeleton ships floating across the sky. That was probably part of their plan. If they had been patient enough to wait for a darker night, they would have fared better, perhaps. But everyone knows that pirates are impatient.

They must have seen the citizens of Nodnol take to the skies in their own airships. Heard the alarms that sounded in the city. But the skeleton ships didn't make a sound.

These ships made no noise whatsoever.

It was one of the strangest things I've ever seen. The ships were sailing so close to one another, you could spit from one and have it land on the other, and the only sound they made was the creak from the old wood as the sails shifted in the wind.

Isolde's face was pale. It was the first time I'd ever seen her show any fear. I was trembling. True, I knew how to navigate my boat in the water, but air is altogether different. Air is moodier, far less forgiving than the sea.

So there was the *Sweet Leroy*, passing near a black ship with black sails. And there I was in my boat, trailing after.

I wanted to yell at Isolde to be careful, but I wasn't going to be the one to break the silence.

Lulu, Janie, and Isolde stood on the deck of the *Sweet Leroy*. About twenty-five pirates were on the deck of the pirate ship. I wondered what its name was. Something sinister, surely.

Not being able to resist, I reduced the air in my envelope and descended. Then I adjusted my sail so I could fly below the pirate ship.

It was the *Dreadful Wellington*.

Well, it got the dreadful part right. But Wellington? That's not scary.

Just as the *Dreadful Wellington* passed, someone let out a battle cry.

Then everyone began to howl.

"Evasive maneuvers!" Lulu yelled as Janie veered their ship to the right. "Isolde, the rigging!"

I wouldn't have thought Isolde knew much about rigging, but she was an admirable first mate.

"You should go, Boy," she yelled over to me. "It might get rough here soon."

"I need to make sure you'll be safe," I yelled back.

That's not part of the rules. But I wanted to anyway.

"You just want to stay around Janie and prove yourself worthy," Isolde called over, laughing.

Since the actual fighting hadn't started yet, there was a moment to joke. There was a lot of teeth gnashing and insult

flinging happening
between the ships.

"Avast, you slimy slugs. You rat-tailed
scallywags," yelled what could only be the
captain of the *Dreadful Wellington*.

The captain, of course, was a she. Her sword sliced
through the air so fast, light couldn't catch the blade. She saw
my shocked face and laughed. The most terrifying laugh I'd ever
encountered. And I sail the Sea all the time. That should tell you
something.

"You'll not be threatening the good people of this city!" Isolde
yelled, standing on the edge of the bow.

"Isolde, get back here!" cried Lulu.

"Ah, let her go, Lulu. She's up for a good fight," said Janie.

"Isolde, NOOOOOOO!" I screamed into the night.

She flashed me a quick smile, then turned away and leaped
over into the *Dreadful Wellington*, brandishing her sword and
crying out, "Which one of you cockroaches is first?"

There was fighting everywhere. Pirates were landing on houses, jumping in and stealing, while others ran through the streets setting fire to whatever they found. The smoke soon surrounded me. I couldn't see where I was going.

It was the most frightened I'd ever been.

The smoke entered my lungs, and I began coughing and coughing. I fell onto the deck of my boat, only to feel something, perhaps an ill-aimed curse, slam into my boat, giving it a hearty shove and sending me spinning far, far away from the fighting.

Far away from Isolde and from Nodnol altogether.

Chapter Sixteen

Once again, the Boy left me with an unfinished story. And though Caragh and I had a million questions, there was only one that really mattered.

How would we get to Nodnol?

The Boy didn't say much about that.

He hemmed and hawed about how difficult it was going to be, even though he wouldn't give any details.

Very strange indeed.

And we'd been on the boat for a good long while—longer than when we traveled to find Caragh's circus.

He was hiding something.

I wanted to talk to the Sea more than ever, but she was having none of it. The waves were becoming fierce, and clouds looming overhead completely blocked the moon. She sloshed us about on the tide—up one wave and down the next. *It is as if the Sea doesn't want us to succeed.*

Caragh screamed from time to time, but the Boy was as calm as a cucumber. We both knew the Sea wouldn't sink us. Deter us, yes. But I didn't think she was allowed to sink the Boy, and I knew she'd never do that. But while she was thrashing about, it was impossible to have any sort of conversation with her.

I needed to speak with her alone. Finding alone time on a small boat occupied by a girl and a boy is nearly impossible.

A wave, not too big, lapped up against the boat.

Perhaps the Sea herself sent it to me. It was perfect.

Soundlessly, I hopped off the edge of the boat and floated on the wave into the blackness of the Sea.

Yes, it was cruel to let Caragh and the Boy think that the Sea took me. But there were more important things to worry about. I'd be back soon enough.

At least I hoped I would.

You might think that rabbits don't know how to swim, but it felt just like when I was a girl and had learned in a pond near our house. And luckily, rabbits are light. I just had to keep my paws moving and my head above the surface.

The water was very cold, and in a few minutes, I was shivering.

I didn't know where I was going, but I had hoped that the Sea (or Murien, or my grandmother, whichever she would like best), would know I was here, paddling in her depths.

Silhouetted against the full moon, the little boat carrying Caragh and the Boy was tossed upon the surf until it was a dark speck against the brilliant white circle, the small storm following their every movement. And then it faded.

I was alone, swimming in the freezing ocean.

Maybe she didn't know I was here.

"Hellooooo," I said to the Sea. "It's me, Albie."

The more I pondered it, the more I just couldn't think of her as my grandmother. Whoever Murien was had dissolved into the waves long ago. Perhaps it was like those stories of Greek gods the Magician read to us, who took human form sometimes. That's what I thought happened with the Magician and the Sea. She became human for a time, had a magical child, and then vanished.

Did the Sea even remember being Murien?

There was silence for a minute. Two minutes.

"Albie, I thought that was you.
Why are you swimming in my waves so blue?"

"Well," I started, but the words wouldn't come. I hadn't really planned how I would start the conversation, and now that I was here, in the big middle of the ocean, I was rather tongue-tied.

> *"Oh, you are not doing what I think you are doing.*
> *Are you?*
> *Please tell me no.*
> *I do not want it to be so."*

At least she was still rhyming.
"Yes, the Boy and I and Caragh are going to rescue Isolde."

> *"Rescue?"*

"We are going to take her back to Cork."

> *"And you think that's what she wants?*
> *That is her wish?*
> *To go back to Cork*
> *And, and . . . flop like a fish?"*

Uh-oh.

That was the worst verse I'd ever heard from the Sea. She must have been pretty flustered.

And I was shivering. My little teeth chattered against each other violently.

"Oh, Albie, I am sorry.
Here you go.
I did not mean
To chill you so."

And upon a wave, small and lilting, floated a white round circle.

A life preserver.

I swam under the edge as the Sea pushed me up through the center. I noticed the faded letters RMS TITANIC.

"Just something I had lying around.
Hold it close, it's safe and round."

"You didn't want the Boy and Isolde to go through the portals to Nodnol? And you don't want us to go back there now?"

The Sea chuckled, gentle and deep.

"Oh, Albie, I would not choose to harm any of you. Not at all.
But there are guardians in the waters, some large and some small."

"Don't you control everything in the ocean?" I asked.

"*No.*"

That one word worried me even more than Hybrasil sinking.

"But there are creatures that we must vanquish?" I asked. "Is this correct?"

> "*The ocean is mine, 'tis true.*
> *But control it? I do not do.*
> *Nature is an unusual beast,*
> *Control is difficult, to say the least.*"

"I really wish you wouldn't rhyme. It makes everything seem a little sillier and less serious than it actually is."

She was quiet then, for a minute. Two minutes. Five minutes. Then she said quietly, ever so quietly,

> "*I am sorry, Albie.*
> *Speaking in verse*
> *Is as close to speaking*
> *Your language*
> *As I can come.*
> *And rhyme is the easiest.*
> *You cannot speak my language.*
> *You do not understand the words of foam*
> *Or the nuances of the waves*

Or the narratives I create
As I splash upon the shore.
The best I can do
Is to make you feel poetry
In your blood
When you look at me.
I apologize
If you find it
Annoying."

There wasn't much I could say, except, "I'm sorry."

She was quiet again, absorbing my apology, and (I think) accepting it.

She finally replied. And for the first time, not in verse.

"I have been trying to keep you away from them, for I cannot help you defeat the beasts, Albie. But I can show them to you. Perhaps that will help you on your journey."

She made a whirlpool then, right next to me, where the center of it was as clear as glass. Then, it became foggy, and a figure appeared.

It was horselike, which was strange, for horses didn't usually swim in the ocean.

"Kelpies," the Sea said. *"Water horses."*

They were lovely, actually, with their pelts an iridescent

black and green. If you just looked at their coats, and the way they shimmered in the water, you'd soon be hypnotized by them. Which was why I looked away.

"Beautiful. Dangerous."

I could see both the loveliness and the deadliness. What I couldn't see was how the Boy and Isolde had survived their encounter with the kelpies.

"You said you can't help us, not really, anyway. Although, I know you'll be watching, of course you will. But if there's anything we can do to—"

> *"The Boy knows, of course.*
> *He did it before.*
> *Now he must return*
> *What he stole."*

The last part shocked me. Apparently, I wasn't the only thief. I stole magic. What had the Boy taken?

Before I could ask, the waves changed direction, and I floated away from the whirlpool and back toward the Boy's boat. I knew it was useless to argue with the Sea—she wanted me to go, and so I would.

But I'd be a liar if I said I wasn't mad about it.

On the horizon, in the shadow of the full moon, I could see the outline of Caragh and the Boy, sitting just a little too close in the boat. The small storm was gone—I guess the Sea knew she was dealing with someone as stubborn as herself. But knowing that didn't make me feel better. A storm was one thing—beasts were another. Soon, I drifted up to the side of the boat, my life preserver barely brushing it. I leaped over the edge, with both elegance and silence.

They hadn't even noticed my absence. They were staring dreamily into each other's eyes.

Ew.

I had to put a stop to this. I made my way to the front and wedged myself right between them. Gave myself a nice shake for good measure, soaking them both.

"Albie!" they cried in unison.

"How did you and Isolde get past the kelpies?" I blurted.

The Boy moved back, startled. Good. "How did you know about the kelpies?" he asked.

"What's a kelpie?" asked Caragh.

I love knowing stuff that I'm not supposed to know. But the look on the Boy's face wasn't as satisfying as I'd hoped. It was a little terrifying.

I'd never seen the Boy lose his wits.

Now he was sweating, which made his hair stick to his head in an embarrassing way.

"Albie, I need to know. How did you find out about them? You went into the Sea, didn't you? What did you find out?"

I paused and looked up at the moon for courage. Then out at the waves for strength.

"I'll tell you. But I'm not the only one with secrets. Maybe you should think about sharing yours before you get us all killed."

"And what secrets do you think I have?"

His voice shook, the teensiest bit. My rabbit ears picked it up. Caragh pulled the scarf the Boy gave her around her head, to keep out the wind, which was whipping in irregular bursts. The storm might have gone, but the wind remained.

"Well, you already told me the island was sinking because of you, but you never told me why. And then there's the fact of your job—I mean, what kind of a boy floats a boat across the ocean to different places and different times? And as for the kelpies, well, we both know there is more to that story, don't we?"

I didn't really *know* there was more to it, but I took a chance.

"If I tell you," he said, looking at Caragh, not me, "you will think less of me. And it will change things. It will change everything."

We were in a small boat getting tossed about, with no idea where we were or how we were supposed to get to where we were supposed to go. A change was what we needed.

"Get on with it, then," I said. "We haven't got all night."

The Boy Speaks:
His Own Story

To know about me, you must first learn about my father.

There are those who think my father is Death himself. That isn't true. Not at all. They say that Death rides a silent chariot—which isn't true, either. At least not all the time.

Sometimes Death rides in a boat. And when he does, my father pilots the boat for him.

My father is called Barinthus. And he is older than time. When King Arthur was slain and floated on a barge to Avalon to await his chance to rule again, it was my father who saw him safely there.

Our family knows the Sea. Every secret the Sea possesses we possess as well.

And so you are asking yourself how is it that a boy, a normal-looking boy, is the son of the Ferryman? He doesn't look—unusual—as one might expect. No, I look incredibly, boringly usual. It is my destiny to fade into the crowd, to see but not be seen.

But you, Caragh, and you, Albie—and each of your rabbit sisters—you *see* me. For whatever the reason, you see me. And I can't tell you how strangely wonderful a thing that is—to be seen. And I would have never had the pleasure of making your acquaintances had it not been for the Magician. And a bargain.

The Magician is better at magic than you can fathom. He has cheated Death for hundreds of years. He has come as close to immortality as any mortal probably ever has. It became a joke, almost, between Death and the Magician, the unstoppable, unkillable Magician.

Until the Magician vanished.

Death knew he was out there, somewhere. He had to be. If he had died, then Death would know. That is his job—his sole purpose.

The Magician was hiding well—on Hybrasil. An enchanted island is the best place to hide from Death, for the rules aren't quite the same as they are elsewhere. Enchantment has its own guidelines.

So, there the Magician was, hiding from Death. But we know the secrets of the Sea, my father and I. And soon, my father told Death where the Magician was.

Death sank the island, and the Magician escaped. Then Hybrasil mysteriously resurfaced, along with the Magician.

My father had been training me because, in the true style of predictable destinies, I will one day be the Ferryman. I go out on my boat, learning the Sea's moods on my own. There won't always be a Barinthus to learn from.

When Hybrasil reemerged, my father didn't notice. Or if he did, he said nothing to me. Perhaps he was too busy. It's an overwhelming job, dealing with the death barge.

So many souls.

As I was learning to navigate the Seas, I stumbled upon Hybrasil, the island that should be on the bottom of the Sea. It was my duty to tell Death of my findings.

But I didn't. I waited, fascinated by my discovery. I wanted to explore, but after a day or two of spying, I realized that magic was afoot, and that I'd stumbled upon a very powerful enchantment. I went to the Magician and told him that I knew. He was deflated, to say the least—not happy to see me at all. He'd never intended to be found, not until he was good and ready. Not until he'd figured out what to do about you rabbit girls.

He was so very tired of holding the island afloat. For it is him, his magic, that has kept the island above the waves all these years. When I found the island, I broke the rather large enchantment that holds the island afloat. It can't be fixed. The

Magician knew his time was limited, but he needed time to see each of you rabbits off into the world. To save you. We made a bargain. I agreed to ferry you girls across the Sea into new lives and he got more time. Once you were away from Hybrasil, it was his hope that the spell that turned you into rabbits would be . . . less binding. Once you choose your destinies and change back into girls, he will sink into the Sea.

And Death will have the trophy that he has sought for so long.

Chapter Seventeen

Caragh was weeping when the Boy finished. There were tears in my eyes, too, but I blinked them back. We cried for different reasons, I'm sure.

The Boy didn't comfort Caragh. He probably thought that she wouldn't want him to. Maybe she hated him now for weakening the Magician—and she didn't even know he was our grandfather yet.

I needed to tell her. Later. In private.

And the Sea had said the Boy stole something and had to return it in order to defeat the kelpies. And if we didn't deal with that, the rest of it wouldn't matter.

"Ahem. Kelpies?" I asked.

No answer.

"The Sea said you stole something."

He reached into his pocket and pulled out a shimmery leather cord fastened together in junctures with small gold rings.

"This."

As he held it in his hands, a horse's bridle, you could see the magic dripping off it.

Dangerous.

"It tames the kelpies. If you put it on their leader, then the herd will follow," the Boy said.

"Where did you steal it from?" I asked.

"Not where, but who," the Boy said sadly. "My father."

The ocean stilled. Even the lapping of tiny waves as they licked the side of our boat quieted.

The Boy looked up at me sheepishly. He still wasn't brave enough to see if Caragh would meet his eye, but I guess a rabbit isn't as frightening as an angry girl.

"He's been busy, see, with the war and

all. There are lots of battles in the Pacific and the Atlantic. Lots of battles mean lots of casualties. Yes, he has been quite occupied."

"The Sea says you have to give it back."

"But if I give it back, I'll never get past them. They are beastly, as I'm sure you know, being such a knowledgeable rabbit."

My mother wasn't one for telling fanciful tales. She didn't believe in princesses with towers or fairy godmothers. She said there was enough real magic in the world to worry about and not to waste time with imaginary magic. But I wonder sometimes, if it's not all the same thing. All I knew about kelpies were things from a book I read in the Magician's library called *Mysterious Creatures*. Inside the dusty pages, I read about faeries who curdled your milk, sluaghs who stole your soul and flew off as birds, and of course, kelpies. Kelpies were a type of horse that lived in water and lured unsuspecting people to get onto their backs with their beautiful flowing manes. If you got on one, it would gallop you away to your death. So I was guessing that Death was their master.

"Well, I'm not returning it," the Boy said. "Not just yet. Not until I use it to get to the portals."

"You mean *we*. *We* are going through the portals."

"No. Too dangerous." His voice was quiet but firm. "You aren't going. Neither of you." He looked like he held even more secrets and they were ready to spill out of him.

"You are *not* the boss," I said.

Caragh, who had been silent this entire time, finally spoke up.

"We've done things your way," she began, her eyes never leaving the Boy's face. "And look where it has gotten us. All my sisters separated by space and time, searching for our destinies. Maybe that isn't how people find their way in life. Maybe we should listen to Albie's idea."

The Boy looked down, then nodded.

"Very well. What's your idea, Albie?"

Good question.

"I need to think," I said.

"Take your time," said the Boy. "I can't wait to hear."

And with that, the Boy pulled his cap down over his eyes and lay back. He folded his hands across his chest just like he was going to sleep.

He started fake snoring.

Caragh yawned big and wide.

"You can take a rest, you know," I said with a sigh. "It's not like I'm going to have some amazing idea and not wake you and tell you about it."

"You should sleep, too," Caragh said, followed by another yawn.

"Oh, I will."

But not yet.

Chapter Eighteen

I didn't seem to need much sleep as a rabbit. The Boy's fake snores turned real soon enough, and Caragh's mouth hung open a little as she fell asleep, too.

Somewhere out there was a portal to Nodnol.

And *I* would be the one going through it. I couldn't let the Boy botch our chance to save Isolde.

Grabbing the bridle from the Boy's pocket was easy, as was silently splashing over the side of the boat. Finding the leader of the kelpies, now that was going to be hard.

The Magician's book said that kelpies hunted in shallow waters, which made it easier to find humans and lure them onto their backs. If kelpies were near the shore, and their job was to guard the portal, it only made sense then that the portal to Nodnol was near the shore as well.

The problem was the current. I don't know much about

how the Sea works, but it seemed to me that the waves took you either toward the land or away from it. So I had a fifty-fifty chance of getting there.

I was floating in the *Titanic* life preserver, which had strangely remained near the Boy's boat. Sometimes it did seem like this rabbit had a little luck.

The waves were loud, but I could've sworn the Howler was nearby. My rabbit fur stood on end, just like it would when the howling would start.

I gritted my teeth and tucked my ears under my chin to block out any noise. No time for Howlers.

I kept my feet from dangling and my tail from dipping into the water. Obviously, I didn't want *her* to know what I was doing. There was no way the Sea would think that meeting up with a herd of kelpies was a good idea.

They call to you, you know. When they can smell you, they start calling. It resembles the worst, most off-key singing. And it echoes, on and on and on.

It was a terrifying sound. My stomach felt swirly and squirmy, and my fur felt like it grew on the inside of my skin.

The Sea was rather rough near the kelpies. Lots of thrashing waves and foam.

The kelpies threw their shadows, tall and gloomy, against the tossing waves. Occasionally, a glimmer of an iridescent green mane slipped into view.

It was mesmerizing.

It didn't take long for them to surround me. Perhaps they were fighting over which of them was going to tempt me on its back and drag me down to the depths.

I needed the leader of the herd. A bold bronze-colored kelpie approached and nudged at my little circle of life, causing it to tip wildly.

But I held on.

Another did the same, and soon, they were bombarding me with their noses. Holding the glimmering bridle in my hand, I threw it over the head of the bronze kelpie, hoping with all my might it was the leader.

Immediately the kelpie I'd bridled slowed his assault. He swam close to me and bowed his head in submission. The rest of them, twelve or so, followed his lead.

They knelt before me on a bed of froth and foam like I was their queen.

Chapter Nineteen

If my mother had been around, she'd have scolded me for getting on the back of a magical creature. She tried to instill in her children proper respect for the magical arts and sciences. For a moment, I thought about how wonderful it would be to have someone scold me to keep me safe.

I think the Sea had discovered what I was up to, for the waves became severe and strange. But I was already on the kelpie's back, whispering *"Nodnol"* into his ear.

Down we dove, down to the bottom of the ocean, the kelpie's green mane tickling my nose. I wasn't gasping for air, which must have been part of the magic of the bridle.

And then there was a light.

And a very grand cavern.

The kelpie hadn't taken me to Nodnol. Not one bit.

I had an awful feeling I knew where I was. After all, where else would a kelpie take its prey but to its leader? And who watched over Death in the Sea?

Before swimming away and leaving me utterly stranded, the kelpie lowered its head and curved its back so I tumbled off. I was still holding the bridle, which slid off with ease.

"Barinthus?" I called, surprised to hear my voice under the waves. Bridle magic again.

"Barinthus!" I shouted fiercely this time. It was like we were no longer underwater, yet I could taste the salt on my tongue and feel the water in the way I moved as if in slow motion.

"What do you want?" The voice was the oldest-sounding thing I'd ever heard. And the most tired. It made the old Magician sound like a spring chicken.

"Speak up! I can't see you!" he commanded.

A figure loomed. Like the Boy, he was meant to blend in. His skin and hair were greenish blue, and his skin wrinkled the way your fingers do if you stay in the tub too long.

"Hulloooo?" I said timidly.

"Where are you?"

"Down here, sir," I said, because for some reason I found myself scampering along the floor of the cave rather than swimming.

The fact that I was holding the bridle gave me only two options. Truth or lie. I am embarrassed to say that I didn't choose truth. However, it wasn't exactly a lie, either. "I'm returning this. It was stolen, I think." I laid the bridle at his feet, which were bare and green, too.

"Did my son send you?" He bent down, picked me up by my ears, and brought me level with his face.

"Not sent. Not really."

He scrunched his eyes at me, like it would help him read my mind.

He let go, and I floated back down to the bottom of the cave. He turned from me and walked to a table, where he laid the bridle absently.

"What do you want?" he asked, taking a seat at the table and motioning for me to do the same.

I hopped up to the chair, then to the table.

Up close, he was even scarier. In the oddly lit room, the shadows gave his face an eerie transparency. The face in front of me was there and not there at the same time.

"I just wanted to give this back. He, um, took it, I think. But he had a good reason. I'm just giving it back."

"And I'm asking you what you want for it."

"Nothing, I guess. Isn't it yours?"

"Of course it's mine!" he roared, slamming his fist on the table, sending me swirling head over ears off the table. I swam back over, trying to stay calm.

"So, as I said, I am bringing it back. We need to pass—"

Barinthus interrupted. "You know nothing, rabbit."

"I know this bridle is yours and that I have returned it," I said. "And my name is Albie O'Brien."

"Is it, now?" he said. "Let me see." He reached out, and a scrolled list appeared in his hand. "Let's see if you are here, Albie." He scanned the incredibly long list in an instant, then turned his gaze back to me. "Well, not on the list. That's a good thing, for you, anyway. It means you're not on the list to die at sea. I'm not destined to ferry you in my boat."

I gulped, somewhat relieved.

"But you know nothing of how the Sea works, do you?"

I shook my head. "Not really, sir."

He seemed to puff up a bit at the *sir*.

"And nothing of life and death, obviously."

Of course I knew about death. My parents were dead. That's about the most horrible lesson a person can have to learn.

"I assume you have noticed that life is not . . . what is the word . . . fair? If you do something good, that doesn't guarantee that something good will happen to you, does it? Bad things happen to good people all the time, don't they, rabbit—I mean, Albie? Things in the Sea are much fairer. When you return something, you must be rewarded. Thus, I must give you something in order for me to take control of the bridle again."

The Sea had a sense of fairness—I would have expected no less.

I couldn't think of anything he had that I might want.

"I can't bring your parents back, if you were wondering that."

I hadn't even thought of that.

"What we need is passage to a place that is neither here nor there, if that makes any sense," I said.

"Who is we?" he asked.

"It's um, me . . . and um, also—"

"Me." It was the Boy. Out of nowhere, he swam over, able to breathe in water. I hadn't seen nor heard him approach.

"Son," said Barinthus.

"Father."

Neither made the move to embrace.

"So you are a thief now as well as a deceptive runaway?"

"I didn't run away. I rowed away in my boat," said the Boy. "Which, as you recall, I'm allowed to do."

"Indeed," said Barinthus. "Surely you realize the danger you have put yourself in."

"I have, all my life, lived in danger."

Barinthus didn't like that last comment one little bit.

He seethed. There was actual smoke coming from his ears! (Later the Boy would tell me it was a trick of the light. And he would also tell me that steam couldn't really exist underwater and that I'd learn about that if I ever studied about matter and chemistry. But I knew what I saw.)

"Maybe never more so than right now, *Son*." His voice was truly menacing now. Why was he so angry? Except for the stealing bit. But nobody's kids were perfect, were they?

Barinthus, still fuming, glanced absently in my direction. "And what about you, rabbit?"

I shrugged. What else could I do?

Barinthus rose and took a step toward his son. One of the Boy's feet moved backward, but slowly the foot moved back to its place, and the Boy held firm. They looked at each other, not blinking.

Finally Barinthus sighed. A long, deep sigh, the kind my mother used to make when she'd find me all messy. "So," he said.

"So," said the Boy.

"I don't have time to deal with this. Do you know what it's like to be the Ferryman during times of war? Well, yes, I suppose you do, because there is always some sort of war going on. That's humanity for you. Capable of such deep love and such deep hatred."

He turned back toward the table and collected the bridle. It was small in his hand, but still shimmery.

"Another day we'll deal with things between us, my son. Another day. I've souls to guide across the abyss. And you have things to do as well. Obligations I trust you haven't forgotten."

"I haven't forgotten."

"Good. We shall reconvene soon."

The Boy nodded. I didn't know if Barinthus meant that I

would be part of that meeting, but I couldn't keep from nodding.

"And, rabbit—Albie—you and whoever else is with you can have safe passage to wherever it is you want to go. No beasts will hinder you. Consider matters between us settled."

The Boy motioned to me that it was time go, so I hopped through the water to him and leaped into his arms.

"Son," Barinthus said, and the Boy turned around. "Don't forget the rules."

"I won't."

"And the next time you want something, how about if you just ask instead of stealing? Hmm?"

Chapter Twenty

Caragh wasn't there when we got back to the boat.

She hadn't left a note, either. Perhaps she was just a little too used to doing things on her own; she had forgotten that other people might care what she'd gotten herself into. It shouldn't have surprised us—her last job was being shot from a cannon.

"She's not dead," the Boy said as he rowed us into darkening skies and even darker waters. "I'd know if she was. That's one of the benefits of being the son of Barinthus, I suppose."

Lucky him.

Looking at the vastness of the Sea, I knew he was right. The Sea wouldn't have taken Caragh into its depths. She just wouldn't have. Which means that, unless she had a mad desire to get shot from a cannon again, she was probably trying to sneak her way to Nodnol.

"How will she get past the kelpies? We gave your father back the bridle."

"Actually, *you* gave him back the bridle."

I wasn't going to argue. The water was getting choppy, and some of the waves were sporting tiny white hats. Festive but deadly.

"There are other ways," he said.

"Like what?"

"My father promised safe passage. Caragh probably got through the portal just fine."

A flash of lightning interrupted our conversation, followed by a crack of thunder.

"That came out of nowhere!" I cried.

"Did it?" said the Boy. He maneuvered his boat up and down the whitecaps with ease.

"Are *you* making that storm?" I cried over the sounds of the Sea and the air.

"What storm?" he asked, smirking. "No," he continued. "I'm not making this storm. Barinthus is."

"Why?" I asked as I rolled in a little ball and careened from one side of the boat to the other, slamming against the side. My ears got smashed, which made my eyes water.

"He's mad."

I gave him a look. Was I really going to have to ask *why* again?

"Okay, well, I took something. I knew he'd cause a big storm. When he does that, the kelpies automatically retreat."

"You stole from your dad *again*?"

"Borrowed," said the Boy, reaching into his pocket and pulling out the bridle. "Besides, this has lots of uses, and it might come in handy."

Another wave washed over the side, nearly whisking me away.

"I'll return it when we're done. Promise."

I thought I'd feel it when we passed through the portal. But one moment there was nothing in front of us, the next, Nodnol loomed ahead. No shift in the wind, no vibration. Just like when my sisters and I landed on Hybrasil in that ratty old boat.

It was late afternoon. We found Caragh just as we approached the shore of the Thames. She was standing on the edge, waiting for us. The Boy tried to flex his muscles as he rowed. Embarrassing.

Caragh's hair was a mess, and her dress was ripped at the hem. One of her high-heeled shoes was missing and had been replaced by a rather sturdy-looking boot. Why didn't she just change into the matching boot that dangled from her hand? Maybe she didn't notice how ridiculous she looked.

When she saw us, her expression brightened; then her eyebrows came together like two trains on a collision course.

"Where have you been? Did you think I wanted to spend the next ten years sitting here waiting for you?" she screeched at us as she scrambled into the boat. "I wouldn't have, I tell you. I should just stay with Isolde, and the two of you can go to the devil."

Wow. She was really, really mad.

"How did you get here? Did you swim?" I asked.

"No. Obviously." She glared at me, huffed, and plopped herself on the wooden bench. She pointed to a large ship overhead with grand sails and a plaque that read BRAVE PADDY on the bottom. *Our father's name.* A rope ladder was slowly lowering just above the Boy's boat. "She came for me. She patrols the portal, you know. A pretty important job."

Isolde's ship cast a shadow, enveloping us in gentle darkness. "We should go. Isolde says there will be another attack soon."

"Pirates, I presume," said the Boy.

"Of course it's pirates."

"Where is Isolde?" I asked. "We can't leave without her."

Caragh softened, replacing mad with sad. She put a hand on my paw ever so softly. "Aw, Albie honey, she . . . well . . . Isolde should tell you herself."

In that moment, the figure of a girl came jauntily down the rope ladder and jumped into the Boy's boat. We rocked back and forth. Caragh and the Boy nearly went over opposite edges.

"Oh, Albie! You foolish little rabbit girl!" She picked me up and twirled me around. "Oh, that I could have someone with your boldness, your courage, your downright sneakiness here on my crew. But alas, that would mean asking you to stay here, and it's far too dangerous for a rabbit girl."

"Aren't you coming with us?" I asked, my trembling voice in danger of getting lost in the rising wind.

"Albie, Nodnol has become a place I can't leave. It's my home. Caragh told me how you're going to create a home for all of us again in Cork—how you're searching across time and place to gather us together, back in that lovely vine-covered cottage. Oh, Albie, only you! Only you could seek to undo your rare and wild curse."

"You knew it was me?"

"Of course. We all knew. Who else would it have been?"

My heart caught. They knew. "Come with us, Isolde. Come home," I begged.

"I don't need to go home to Cork because I already am home. You see, some people are always longing for the one place that feels right. Then there are those of us who carry our home with us wherever we go. I'm always home. And I don't need a rescue from this foul and violent place—I've become a rescuer. Saving others from the scourge of pirates in the sky is what I was born to do."

I might have cried a little.

"Don't be sad, Albie, and don't get angry, either. We all know where that can lead. You don't get to control everyone's life and change it just because you want to. You tried that before, and look what happened."

"You're not mad at me—for turning you into a rabbit?"

"Of course not. It was an adventure. I do so love adventures."

She kissed the top of my head and dropped me not so gently to the deck of the Boy's boat. She hugged Caragh one last time, gave the Boy a wink and was up the rope ladder and sailing off on the *Brave Paddy* before I could stop her.

She was right, of course, about trying to control everyone's life.

Maybe I should just admit it. This idea was stupid. I couldn't save my parents. I couldn't save the island. I couldn't save the Magician. And now I couldn't unite my sisters.

Caragh and the Boy were still looking at me, so I sniffed and wiped my nose with my paw.

"To Rory, I guess."

The birds, silhouetted against the setting sun, squawked their consent.

Not that I cared what stupid birds thought.

"To Rory," the Boy repeated.

There was really no place else to go.

The Boy Speaks:
The Story of Rory

Rory knew just where she wanted to go, and it wasn't a difficult place to find, which makes her story rather short. I hope you'll see that not everything is ringmasters and pirate airships.

The ocean was gentle as it took us the short distance to Cork.

That's all Rory wanted. She just wanted to go home.

(*Caragh's eyes widened. Mine did, too. Caragh didn't know this was also part of my wish.*)

"You're sure?" I asked Rory. "I mean, you could go anywhere in the world, any time. There's a lot out there to explore. Are you certain that you just want to go back to Cork? They won't be there, you know. Your parents are . . . gone."

Rory was a quiet sort, so she just nodded.

She was, though, a little hesitant about turning back into a girl.

"What if I don't remember how to be a girl?" she asked. "It's been such a long time."

"Not really that long," I said as the boat glided across the crystal-blue waves. Some days are like that, you know? Where the Sea is almost showing off. Some days the Sea truly wants you to appreciate how beautiful it is.

(Yes, that sounded like the Sea I knew.)

"Besides, how hard can it be to be a girl?" I asked.

"Well, that is a very horrible type of question. You realize how horrible it sounded, don't you, Boy?" Rory said.

I replayed my response in my head. Yes, I suppose you could take it the wrong way.

"It's harder to be a girl than to be a rabbit. Just think about that for a minute."

So I did.

Finally, when even the water that lapped up against the side of the boat was almost silent, she spoke again.

"I just want to be good at this, that's all."

"You'll be fine," I said, trying my best to be encouraging.

"We'll see."

The house in Cork was monstrously overgrown. It was like every gardener in Ireland had not only refused to work there, but had dumped their weeds there, too.

It was so covered in vines that it almost didn't look like a house.

"How long since you've been here?"

"Since before the Blitz," Rory said.

Two years, more or less.

She scampered about the yard, sniffing madly.

I supposed that everything must have smelled different. However, I'm guessing that not having been a rabbit in Cork, she wasn't certain herself how it smelled in the past.

"It smells . . . strange," she said.

"Let's go in, shall we?"

Rory refused to transform, but that was all right. She'd do so in her own time.

The door to the house was open.

Not a good sign.

Rory and I exchanged a look. What if we found a stranger in the house and had to throw him out? I was sure that an undersized Boy and a scrawny rabbit weren't any match for a squatter.

We crept inside, the door not even creaking as we slipped past.

I'm not certain what your home looked like when you were last there, but I can almost guarantee that you wouldn't have recognized it. It had been ransacked. The table and chairs were turned over, cupboards opened, but there was nothing inside, of course. Whatever had been of any value in that house was now completely gone.

(The most valuable things were not things at all. They left before the Blitz.)

Most likely, during the worst of the war, people needed things and were afraid they couldn't get them. And your house had been abandoned so . . .

At least that's what I think happened.

Rory scampered up the stairs. I thought she might be transforming (it seems to be something people like their privacy for) so I waited downstairs, examining bits of broken crockery and such. I checked the fireplace. It had been a long time since there'd been a fire, which I took as a good sign. Perhaps there weren't squatters after all.

"Rory!" I called out. "Everything okay?"

She didn't respond.

I made my way up the staircase to find Rory, still a rabbit, sitting in what must have been her room, for there was a bed frame—no mattress, though—and rosebuds painted on the walls.

Rory was crying.

"It's all right," I said. "It's going to be all right."

"It will never be all right again," she said. "Why can't it be the way it was?"

"Time doesn't move that way. It doesn't go backward," I said.

"Are you sure?" asked Rory.

The truth of it was that I didn't know how time worked. Does anyone? Of course, there are scientists who are quite knowledgeable about space and time and how it all fits together. But I didn't know much about that. I just knew how to navigate the seas.

However, this isn't my story. It belongs to Rory.

"You don't have to stay here," I said. "You haven't chosen all the way. I can take you anywhere else you want to go."

She was quiet for a moment, then sniffled back the last of her tears.

"What place is there for me but home?"

We gathered leaves to sleep on, making beds for ourselves downstairs by the fireplace. She still hadn't changed, but I felt confident she would, soon.

I heard her awaken at midnight. She shook off the leaves from her fur and ever so quietly, sneaked out of the cottage.

I followed, naturally. Rory went to the small woods behind the house. A squirrel came out from a tree and introduced himself to Rory.

"Evening, miss. My name is Bann." He bowed deeply. Squirrels are more polite than you might think.

Rory might have curtsied, but I couldn't tell, since I was hiding behind a tree, trying very hard to be invisible. You might be wondering how I understood squirrel language. The truth is that I had never heard squirrel language before. I think perhaps because Rory understood, I could understand it, too.

Or maybe some other sort of magic was going on. I didn't think about that possibility, but I should have.

An owl swooped down over Rory's head. "I'm Hecate," she said.

And there I was, understanding the words of an owl, too.

I almost called out to Rory, for owls have been known to make a meal of rabbits. But Rory was a large rabbit, and Hecate was a small owl, so I supposed everything could be fine.

"Well, I'm Rory. I used to live here when I was a girl. Before I became a rabbit," Rory said.

"Ah, it's you that smells of magic, then!" Bann scampered up to a low branch, a few below where Hecate sat.

"I remember those girls," the owl said. "My, that was a long time ago."

"You're not planning on staying, are you?" asked Bann. His squirrel eyes were wide and panic-stricken. He was a worrier, that one.

"I was. I mean, I am," said Rory.

"That's not a very good idea," said Hecate. "Others have taken over the house. They aren't very kind, if you must know. I don't think they'll approve of having a rabbit in their house, unless it's in their pot, if you get my meaning."

I didn't think these were the kinds of folks we wanted to deal with. I longed to tell Rory. Privately.

"They don't seem to be here now," said Rory. "Maybe they've gone for good."

Bann snorted. "I doubt that. Probably just robbing other people's houses."

"Oh," said Rory.

"Now, don't you worry your fluffy head about it," said Hecate. "You'll find the woods a friendly place for a rabbit such as yourself. Rarely do we have any wolves or foxes come for a visit, and, since everyone in the woods minds their manners, you'd never have a wolf at your tree unexpected."

"Stay? Here? In the woods?" Rory stumbled to get the words out.

When she wanted to come back to Cork, I doubted it was so that she could live in the woods as a rabbit behind what once was her house.

She looked back at me then. She had to know I was there. I flattened myself against a tree, a lot of good it would do me. Rabbits and their ears!

"Would you excuse me, Bann and Hecate? It was ever so nice to meet you. I'm sure we'll be talking soon." Rory curtsied, then hopped to where I was standing.

"You're about as discreet as a herd of buffalo. And eavesdropping is horribly rude," she said.

"Yes, of course you're correct," I said.

She hopped in front of me, back to the house.

Sheepishly I followed.

There were no squatters inside when we got there. Just our pitiful leaf beds, which didn't make the idea of going back to sleep any more appealing.

"So," I said.

"So," she said.

Silence sat between us like an old grandmother knitting a scarf for an elephant, which is to say, things were quiet between us for quite some time.

"So," I tried again.

"You won't talk me out of this, Boy. This is my home. I'm staying. I'll become friends with all the animals of the woods if I need to, and they'll help me fight off the squatters. Then, and only then, will I change back. So you can go."

It wasn't a bad plan. It would put me off schedule, though, and the Magician wouldn't be happy about that.

"But—"

"No buts," she said. "I'm sorry you'll have to stay so long, but this is the only way I can see to do it."

And so it was. We stayed in the house for several days, clearing out the leaves, branches, and other things that had taken residence within the walls. Your house was ever so creaky. I'd hear noises upstairs, like steps upon the floorboards, and bolt up there only to find not a trace of anyone or anything. Houses settle, I've heard. I just hadn't spent much time in an actual house to recognize it.

We didn't see the squatters once.

And when I say that we cleared out the house, I really mean

that *I* cleared out the house. A rabbit, though fast and clever, isn't helpful with things that require hands.

Rory made friends with other animals outside while I worked. Not just Bann the squirrel and Hecate the owl, but also a weasel named Wat. None of them ever spoke directly to me, although they had to have seen me working my fingers to the bone each day, trying to make the house livable again. They ignored me altogether, pretending that I didn't even exist.

At first I didn't mind. But after a bit, I did.

Feeling invisible is rather . . . horrible.

Everyone wants to be seen.

On the day when we (ahem, I) had finished painting the inside walls with a new coat of whitewash, and had pulled all of the weeds from against the house and burned them in a bonfire, I asked Rory if she was finally ready.

She was about to answer me when we heard it.

It was an animal noise—a loud one. The kind that makes the ground beneath your feet vibrate.

That type of sound gives a person a chill.

"Is that . . . are those . . . sheep?" Rory said, peering through the window as the last dollop of sun disappeared over the hill.

"Sounds like sheep to me," I said.

"Those are some angry-sounding sheep."

She was right. I'd thought if indeed there were sheep, they

would be friendly sheep, like the owl, the squirrel, and the weasel. Those were kind animals.

What was the problem with the sheep?

They rushed the front door.

"If we don't let them in, I think they'll break it down," I said. "Then we'll have to fix it and be even further behind schedule."

Rory agreed. She hopped over to the door, jumped up and opened the latch, and pushed it open with her hind legs.

The sheep slowed down.

There were three of them. It sounded like a hundred, but there were only three.

They nosed their way through the door.

"Hey, who ruined everything? We had things set up so's we'd like it," said one of the sheep.

"Yeah. Looks like a dog's breakfast in here. That's not a good thing, you know," said another one of the sheep.

The largest sheep was silent. He surveyed the place. His black eyes locked onto Rory for a moment, then moved on to me.

He started toward me.

I don't know if there were sheep anywhere near your house in Cork or not, Albie. I'm thinking that it's probably impossible to live in Ireland for a while and not have some sort of relationship with sheep, though I could be wrong. But these sheep, well, they were the kind that called the shots. The kind that terrified shepherds and sheepdogs alike.

Rory was frightened by their size, I could tell. It had been a long time since they were trimmed, and the wool flowed off them like waterfalls. No, that's not quite it. They were like thunderclouds. And dingy gray, too, for these sheep were not clean.

"So," said the first sheep. "Hurry along. Out with you. Find your own cottage."

I was tempted to do just what that sheep said. But Rory said, "This is my cottage. My family's cottage. And I'd appreciate it if you left."

The sheep started laughing. Not a pleasant sound.

"Who ever heard of a rabbit owning a cottage?" they laughed.

"I think it's more likely a rabbit would have a house than a sheep. Especially if you consider the intelligence level . . ." Rory left that dangling. She didn't like insulting people, or animals. It wasn't in her nature.

The sheep glared. Did you know that a sheep's eyes turn red when it is angry? It's true. Red, glowing and demon-like. I've seen many frightening things in my life, but those three sheep from Cork were among the most frightening.

"Baa, baa, black sheep, have you any wool?" the first sheep sang in a growly voice. Made the hairs on my arm stand up.

"No!" said Rory. "I do not have any wool! And you're not going to either if you don't leave this house right now!"

A rabbit, no matter how angry, is still just a rabbit.

"And what are you going to do about it, sweetheart?" said the second sheep.

Rory jumped up on the table so she could be above the sheep. "Have you never heard of the Demon Hare?"

Her voice was a hiss of steam. I'll admit it. I was impressed.

The sheep laughed. "If it's anything like a black sheep, luv, you're still going to get sheared."

"I am the Demon Hare. I am the messenger." Her voice sounded odd. Not like her own.

The sheep laughed louder.

That didn't stop Rory.

She stood on the table, looking down at the sheep, pointing her paw at them.

"Yes. I *am* the Demon Hare. And I *am* the messenger," she said, her voice only a whisper that flew around the room, then floated out the window into the dark of the night.

"Messenger of what?" the sheep said, exasperated.

It was silent. It seemed like she wasn't going to answer.

But of course, she did.

"I am the messenger of Death," she said.

That shut those sheep up quick, I can tell you.

It shut me up, too. Because I knew she was lying. First, she was a rabbit who was really a girl. Second, well, you know about me and Death.

But she spoke with conviction.

The sheep were shaking.

"You know that to mess with me is to mess with . . ." She didn't need to say the last word, but she said it anyway. "Death." She drew out the *th* a bit.

"And even if it's not your time, if you annoy the messenger, then I can make . . . changes." She spoke slowly like it tasted too good on her tongue to let it go. "You wouldn't want that, would you?"

The sheep shook their heads.

It was beautiful the way this small hare had petrified these mean sheep. I'd never seen anything like it. I'd heard that Rory was such a great caregiver. It made me realize that everyone who'd ever said that the worst thing you can do is to anger a mother were absolutely correct.

In a blink, the squatter sheep were gone.

"That was spectacular!" I said eventually.

But Rory just sat there, on top of the table, looking exactly like the rabbit she'd claimed to be, the messenger of Death. You remember the books the Magician read to you, don't you? *Watership Down* with that creepy Black Rabbit of Inlé? I supposed Rory did, too.

"Rory?" I said.

She said nothing.

"Rory!" I said.

Slowly she turned toward me and hissed.

I was more than a little worried.

I skulked along the edges of the room to the door and quickly fled to the woods behind the house.

"Bann? Hecate? Wat?" I called.

Only the night breeze answered me. And I couldn't understand the language.

"Please!" I called. "It's Rory, she needs help!"

I heard a rustling.

Please, please, please let it be someone who will help, I thought.

"I'm friends with Rory!" I called again.

There was more rustling, and maybe whispering. At least, I was hoping there was whispering.

Then, without speaking to me at all, the squirrel, the owl, and the weasel made their way to the house.

They shut the door behind them.

I tried the handle. Locked.

I wondered how four animals without hands would be able to lock a door.

Magic has a smell, you know. Just like the animals said.

And there were all sorts of magical smells coming from the house.

And then there was a voice inside the house.

"Well done, rabbit," it said. I raced back over to the window. "I'd been wondering how to get rid of those nasty sheep. And look, you and the lad cleaned up the place for me."

The voice was as crackly as an old piece of paper, and the person it came from looked old and crackly as well. I'd not seen her in the house before, not at all. She was . . . creepy. She looked like a witch—not a magical person like your mother, but an ancient warty trickster, with eyes so tiny, they almost weren't there. And the way she reached out and pet Rory gave me the shivers. I beat on the window to get Rory's attention, but the blind slid down.

Then all of the blinds were closed.

I yelled and yelled for Rory.

A voice answered my calls. Maybe. It rode the wind, but it wasn't the voice of the wind. It was Rory's voice, but at the same time it wasn't.

"Go away, Boy. I don't need you anymore. Go home."

So I left.

Chapter Twenty-One

"You left her there?" I cried. *"You just went home and left her?"*

"She said she didn't need me, so I left, but I didn't go home," he said. "I'm not allowed to go *home* until . . . well, let's just say there are things I have to do first. And, Albie, you fall into that category."

I wasn't ready for him to change the subject from poor Rory. Still a rabbit, and maybe captured by some witch, this seemed unlikely, but I don't think the Boy had much reason to lie.

And there was something familiar about the way he described that witch.

I really hoped that Bann, Hecate, and Wat were able to help Rory.

My heart was so heavy.

Caragh sighed and shook her head.

The Boy said, "So, pretty much I'm a failure in my mission

to ferry you rabbits to your destinies. Albie, you're the last one, my last chance. And you've got this cockamamie idea that your destiny is to get all your sisters together, save the island, and rescue the Magician. The island is already sinking. You felt it. It can't be saved. Your plan is unreasonable. You have to agree."

I didn't say what was in my mind to say, which was *no*. The word just sat there, like a lump in my throat.

I just wanted . . . I just wanted someone to hold me.

I looked at the Boy. I'd never seen him so down.

Caragh was on the verge of tears again.

Sometimes a person needs a hug.

And sometimes a person needs to give a hug.

Without words or intention, we all ended up in a hug.

And though I'd never admit it to the Boy, that hug was everything I needed.

"Rory might not be like you remember," said the Boy.

The wind and waves had picked up as we neared Cork. This I *had* expected. This was a little message from the Sea, I was certain. She didn't think I should go back to Cork. That much was clear. But it didn't matter. Rory was there, so that was where we needed to go.

Once we'd landed and made our way through the village and up the hill to our cottage, I could hear it.

The Howler, but this time it was different. Softer, more sinister.

Stop following me!

"I know that sound," Caragh said. "I remember it from the island. It started when you turned us into rabbits."

I had a very bad feeling.

"I see you've brought your friend," said the Boy, covering his ears as the howling went from a whistle to a moan.

"It's not my friend!" I yelled.

The Boy walked up to the house.

My house.

"Can you peek in a window or something?" I asked, being too small to do so myself.

But the Boy didn't move. And as far as I could see, all the blinds were still drawn.

"Should we knock?" Caragh asked.

You wouldn't know it to look at me, but every single one of my hairs was standing on end. The Boy reached for the doorknob and turned it without knocking. It was locked.

"Well, I would have locked it, too," said Caragh.

Caragh knocked on the front door. "Rory? Rory? Are you there? It's me, Caragh."

The howling got louder.

Caragh stepped back.

"Something bad is going on in there," I said even as I scampered off to the back of the house.

I knew what I had to do. The only person getting inside of that house was going to be me.

I hid behind the house, willing myself to change back into a girl.

"Albie? Where'd you go?" I heard Caragh calling from the front of the house, but I didn't stop to answer.

I also didn't change.

I remained a cursed rabbit. But that wasn't going to stop me.

At the back of the house there was a small lead-paned window we always called the faerie window. Mum said we were being ridiculous, but we always kept it open so as not to insult any faeries who might want to visit. And it was still, just a crack, but I managed.

Once inside, the howling was more of a whistling, like an angry teakettle. I was going to call Rory's name, but the rabbit part of me thought to stay quiet.

We rabbits are quite good at being quiet.

I scampered down from the window ledge as if my paws were made of marshmallows.

"Albie, I've been expecting you. What on God's green earth took you so long?"

Rory was a girl again. But my big sister was supposed to be bigger than me (if I was a girl), but she wasn't. There was no way on *God's green earth* that she was supposed to be that small. Or frail-looking. Her hair, which she had always brushed until it shone, was tangled and scraggly on her narrow shoulders.

"Rory, what happened to you?"

She smiled sadly and spread her thin arms wide. "Happy Christmas, Albie."

Not only was my sister the size of an eight-year-old (she was twelve now, for goodness' sake!), but the room looked like Christmas. There were garlands of pine and other evergreens intertwined with branches decked with ruby berries and leaves.

"It's been ages since we had Christmas."

I felt the heat behind my eyes. One of my last memories of Mum was that horrible Christmas in London without Papa, and then we lost her a few days later. She'd tried to make it happy for us, even though we spent so many nights down in the shelter.

"Come, come. Would you like some tea?" Rory looked too weak to lift a spoon, and the teakettle shook as she set it on the stove and lit the fire beneath it. "Do sit down. I've been waiting ever so long to see you again." She sat at the table, catching her breath from the tea-making effort.

"Are you okay, Rory? You seem sort of . . ." I didn't want to say *sick*, even though she did look sick, because I didn't want it to be true.

"Oh, I'm fine."

The howling had faded to a soft and mournful cry. I could almost ignore it. Almost.

"Do you hear that noise, Rory?" I asked.

"Hmm . . . Yes, I hear something . . . something. It reminds me of the island. Are you alone?"

How had I forgotten about Caragh and the Boy? "No! Oh, Rory! I'm not here alone, I brought Caragh!"

"Is she making that noise, then?"

I scampered down from the proper chair I'd been sitting in and leaped up to the front door with all my might.

"Here, let me help you with that, dearie." The voice was directly behind me, nearly breathing in my ear.

It wasn't Rory.

I jumped, of course, which is only natural for a rabbit, or anyone who's just had the pants scared off them, I suppose. Not that I was wearing pants.

Whoever was behind me started laughing. Or cackling. Yes, it was definitely a cackle.

"Oh, you should have seen the look on your face!" The cackling turned into wheezing. And how could they see the look on my face from behind me?

"Albie, this is Bronagh. You remember Bronagh, don't you?" said Rory.

I remembered her, all right, though I'd not seen her since she made us leave London and journey to Hybrasil.

Bronagh was maybe even older than the Magician, or so the wrinkles on her face seemed to say. And though she spoke like she still had all her teeth, I couldn't really tell because her mouth was so ancient and puckered, it hid everything.

Her eyes were black and tiny, like a crow's or some other type of nasty bird, except that they hinted at purple in the firelight.

"Pleased to make your acquaintance. Again," she said, bowing to me sarcastically.

Bronagh was more awful than I remembered.

"What are you doing here?" I asked. Things were not at all right in Cork.

Bronagh and I sized each other up for a good long time.

"Why, Albie, don't be rude! Bronagh is our guest."

Bronagh gave me a smug look.

Rory continued, "We're going to have Christmas."

"But it's not Christmas, Rory."

"Oh, Albie. Of course it is."

I didn't really know if it was Christmastime or not. It was a summery day when the Boy and I had left Hybrasil—but most days on Hybrasil were summery. Here the air was heavy with the scent of pine.

At that moment, I remembered Caragh and the Boy waiting at the front door. I scampered over, but of course I couldn't reach the latch.

"Bronagh, do be a dear and open the door for Albie. She'll never manage it otherwise."

Bronagh hobbled over to the door dramatically. Still smirking.

She opened the door, and Caragh flew in, racing to Rory. "Oh my dear, dear Rory! Is everything all right? I was so worried!"

She grabbed our sister in a long embrace. (Rory hadn't embraced me.) They hugged forever. When they finally let go, Caragh went up to Bronagh and said, "Oh, Miss Bronagh, thank you for looking after my sister."

"'Twas nothing," she said.

Ugh.

Rory and Caragh, on the other hand, were oblivious, lost in their own conversation.

Then I noticed that Caragh came in without the Boy.

Scampering over, I tapped her foot and asked about him.

"I don't know where he is, but he didn't want to come in."

A strange sensation came over me as I was scooped up by the ice-cold hands of Bronagh. "Let's get you cleaned up," she whispered to me, her voice close to a snake's hiss. I jerked around and flailed gracelessly to the floor.

"Seriously, Albie, you look more like a drowned rat than a

rabbit. The salt water from the ocean has made your fur stiff and clumpy. Let Bronagh help you. She'll brush you out nice and fine," Rory said from the kitchen as I scurried in behind her.

I raced up the stairs, dodging Bronagh.

"Come back here, *little sister*," Bronagh shrieked after me, but I didn't look back. I could only think about going forward, up those stairs, as fast as rabbitly possible.

Chapter Twenty-Two

I'm not sure what I expected to see in my room. I'd never been the tidiest of girls, nor was I very good at packing—I'd left my favorite slingshot behind, after all—so I wouldn't have been surprised to be greeted by a huge mess.

But everything was quite clean. Too clean.

Every trace of me had been removed.

"I didn't think you'd mind sharing with Bronagh," Rory called up from downstairs.

"Bronagh?" I squeaked out.

"Yes," said the evil hag from right behind me. "We'll be roommates."

"What are you even doing here?" Rude, but I didn't care.

"Oh, little rabbit, look how filthy you are!" she said, trying to reach for me, but if I was too fast to be caught by the Boy, I was much too quick to be snatched by an old lady.

"I asked you a question." I tried to make my voice steely, a rabbit who meant business.

Rory answered breathlessly, having just come up the stairs.

"Bronagh was here when I came home. She'd come to check on the house for us, isn't that kind of her? But then there was that problem with the sheep. She'd been so afraid, she'd bolted herself up in your room. The Boy and I hadn't even noticed her."

Bronagh smiled like she was some sort of angel.

"I didn't know about your mother's gift with magic then," Bronagh said. "But I do now. I discovered some things while poking around. When dear Rory showed up as a rabbit, then changed into a girl, I knew she could use my help."

How dare she *poke* my mother's things!

"I picked this room because of the view," she said. "I've gotten quite used to it. I tidied your things and put them in the closet. I hope you don't mind."

"Of course she won't," Rory answered for me. "Now, I've got things to do, much to get ready. Come on, Bronagh." And with that, they left my room and went back downstairs.

Except it wasn't really *my* room anymore, was it? I took my muddy paws and jumped all over *my* bed. Ha!

This wasn't the reunion with my sisters I had planned.

I had imagined it often enough. All four of us back at our

house. Together. We'd remember Mum and Papa and create a new life where they were never forgotten. And we'd have the Magician there as well. He'd sit in a rocking chair and tell the others how he was really their grandfather, and I'd pretend not to know so as not to ruin the surprise.

And we'd live . . . happily ever after.

But so far, Rory didn't seem that happy to see me. No hugs.

✳ ✳ ✳

No one noticed as I crept down into the parlor, behind the sofa.

"It's not her," said the creaky voice of Bronagh.

"Who?" said Caragh.

"The rabbit isn't your sister. If she was, she would have turned into a girl by now, wouldn't she?" she whispered.

"She's just not ready," said Caragh.

"Or she can't because she's not your sister," said Bronagh. "Even Rory doubts her."

"Albie would have changed," said Rory.

"Maybe Albie chooses not to."

As happy as I was that Caragh was defending me, I had to admit I was bugged. Why hadn't I been able to change yet? Of course, I tried again, there behind the sofa. Unsuccessfully.

"I've learned about these things," Bronagh said, her voice somewhat threatening. "You'd be wise not to cross me."

"And you'd be wise not to cross me." Caragh's voice was low and ice-cold. "I've been bullied once in my life, hauled around by my ears and forced into labor. I'll never, not ever, be told what I can or cannot do by the likes of you."

Caragh huffed off, up the stairs, and slammed the door for good measure.

"She'll come around," Rory said.

"Leave it to me," the evil hag said. With her slumped shoulders and oversized sleeves, she looked like some sort of ancient bird.

I waited for them to go back into the kitchen so I could make my escape. Not that I knew where I was going. Not really, anyway. But I needed to talk to the Boy.

You would have thought I'd have expected the old woman to sneak up behind me and grab me by my ears. But a person, even a smart rabbit person, is sometimes at their dumbest when they are trying to convince others of how smart they are.

Quick as a faerie's whip, Bronagh hefted me up and rushed me to the door of the cottage.

"I won't let you ruin this for me," she hissed. "I read your mother's journals. I know about you girls, *especially you*, and your magic." Then she threw me out the door and called, "You'll be lucky if I don't do worse to you or your sisters before this is over. If you ever come back, I will!"

With that, she slammed the door.

Outside, the howling was deafening. It was worse here than it had ever been on Hybrasil. This was a screechy sort of howl—the kind that itched your teeth and made the inside of your ears ache.

The Howler followed me from Hybrasil to Caragh's circus, across the sea, and to Cork. But how?

If I had thought the Boy would be standing around the outside of the house waiting for us to remember him, I would have been wrong. He was a person of action.

Where would a person of action go?

That's what I was wondering as I hid in some nearby bushes. I needed Bronagh to think I was gone.

I tried not to think about the fact that my sisters were still inside with her. Or that they didn't stop her from getting rid of me. Were they under a spell? Was I the only one who seemed to notice?

I shook to toss off the bad feelings. I had to get away from the howling, so I scurried off toward the forest.

As a girl, I was both delighted and frightened by the forest near our house. The trees were enormous, which meant they made tremendous shadows at nightfall. And everyone knows that shadows are for things that lurk.

But as a rabbit, I wasn't scared of the forest. I'd learned

how to use my spectacular ears to avoid anything that might harm me. But now my ears were filled with the howling, and my old fears enveloped me as I approached the trees.

The howling quieted, though, as I got farther away from the house. I went into the forest until I couldn't hear it at all.

"Hellooo?" I called. Surely the Boy was close. If not him, perhaps those forest creatures he'd met back when he brought Rory here—Bann the squirrel or perhaps Hecate the owl.

I searched the treetops and skies for a sign of either of them. In my distracted state, I tripped over a weasel hole and nearly fell in.

"What's the meaning of this?" asked the weasel upon whose head I was now standing.

"You wouldn't be Wat, would you?" I asked.

"I am indeed," said Wat, slowly, gently rising out of the hole so as not to dump me over.

"I'm looking for a boy," I said. "He came here once before, with Rory. He said he met you, and I thought he might have come to pay a visit."

I had removed myself from Wat's head as gracefully as possible, which wasn't easy.

"You didn't go in that house, did you?" he asked.

"I did."

"You're a brave hare."

"I had to go in. Rory is my sister. Families stick together," I said with all the confidence I could muster.

"Well, we in the forest have a different idea of what comprises a family. A family can be wherever you make it. A family can be whomever you choose."

"That's very philosophical, and I'd love to talk more, but I really need to find the Boy."

The rustling in the bushes let me know that he'd been listening the whole time.

"What is it, Albie?" the Boy asked.

"Oh! So this is Albie!" said Wat jubilantly, then quickly changing to despair. "Oh . . . then . . . this isn't good."

"You've got to get back in there, Albie," said the Boy. "You're the only one who can help them now."

Easy for him to say. He wasn't just tossed aside like a piece of garbage by a woman so horrible that even witches wouldn't have her.

"I'm sure she won't let me back in." I didn't say who *she* was. I didn't have to.

"Threw you out, did she?" the Boy asked.

I nodded.

"Well, you're in good company, then. I suspect she wouldn't have even let me in at all. It's probably best if she doesn't know about me altogether. The element of surprise will be our best ally."

"How do you know her?"

"I don't know her personally, but I know of her. She's one of many. She's a *sluagh*."

"A what?"

He paused, looking at me, then at Wat, as if he was making sure that it was okay to tell us. "Death isn't the only thing that wishes for lives to end. They are spirits so terrible that the afterlife won't have them. A sluagh is a stealer of souls."

"What are you talking about? She's just an old bat who works for the Orphan Removal Society who came to Cork and *stole our house!*"

"And wouldn't that be the perfect occupation for someone looking for souls to steal? Poor little orphans with no one to save them? I've no doubt she was attracted to your sadness. Things are not always exactly what they seem. For heaven's sake, Albie, you're a rabbit who is really a girl! Bronagh is an old woman who is really a sluagh. Don't underestimate her. A sluagh can burst into a flock of birds if that is her wish. Very powerful, that type of magic."

All at once I remembered reading about sluaghs in one of the Magician's books, and also how the boat that took us from London had been surrounded by birds that bombarded us. *Was that Bronagh?* I had known there was something truly horrible about her back then. But I just thought she was a bad person. Bad people exist, I'm sorry to say.

The Boy continued, "Or maybe she's just a thief, and you're right. You can call the constable and have her removed—and you'll have to explain why you're a rabbit, why there aren't other adults around, and answer a whole lot of questions. And then be shipped off to live with some other family."

He was being dramatic, but he also might be right. Involving the authorities would spell disaster for my plans for the family.

"That is the best-case scenario. If I'm right, Albie, her plan isn't to have just the house but your souls as well."

Wat the weasel scurried over to the Boy and crawled up his arm, quickly settling on his shoulder like they were old friends. "You've got to get rid of her," he whispered rather loudly in the Boy's ear. "Banish her once and for all."

"I can't. I can't interfere. Albie has to do it."

"How?"

The Boy paused. His silence lasted what seemed like days. "That's something Albie has to figure out."

Chapter Twenty-Three

Getting rid of the sluagh would require magic. I was rubbish at spells—clearly—but I was going to have to do something and not muddle everything up again. The safety of my family depended on it.

I'd need help from the best magician I knew—Mum. I knew she kept detailed notes on her work in the gorgeously bound journals that sat on top of the tall bookshelf in my parents' room. The very ones that the old hag claimed to have read.

I'd have to sneak back into the house.

Crouching beneath the kitchen window, the Boy and I waited as day melted into night, listening as Bronagh continued to try to turn Rory and Caragh against me.

"If she were really your sister," the hag hissed, "she'd have changed. Why would a girl want to be a rabbit? No, she's just an ordinary hare. She's trying to trick you into sharing this house with her! You're not too stupid to see it, *are you?*"

If there was one thing Caragh hated, it was being thought of as stupid.

I wanted to go dashing in and thump Bronagh with my strong haunches, but the Boy held me back. "Just listen. We must make a plan."

"She hasn't been here that long, but oh, the damage she's done," said Wat. "Things were getting back to normal since Rory got rid of the sheep. She weeded the garden and planted vegetables. Then out of nowhere, the sky turned dark in the middle of the day, like a big shadow was crossing the sun. The next time I saw Rory, she looked ill. And there was that old lady directing her every move. Oh, I know, she says that she's *helping* Rory, but it doesn't look like it. She made Rory put out poison so we don't get too close to the house—as if we'd be stupid enough to eat poison. Bronagh threatened all of us with a big cooking pot if we tried to interfere. *Interfere with what?* We wanted to ask, but we didn't, of course. One doesn't ask an evil hag questions and live, now, does one?"

No, one does not. My ears drooped.

I peered into the kitchen window as the sun sent its last glimmer over the tops of the trees. Caragh was placing a large bowl of water on the floor in front of Bronagh for her to *soak her feet*! Rory brought her a cup of tea and a little chocolate biscuit—*my favorite*! The hag beamed up at my sisters, who smiled back at her. Then, most repulsive of all, they all hugged like Bronagh was a *member of the family*!

That's when the howling started again.

How I hated the Howler.

"What am I supposed to do?" I cried. "It's not like I'm the Magician. I'm just a girl who failed at a spell and who is now a rabbit. A rabbit who failed at a task and is now sitting under a window of what used to be her house with a bunch of other failures."

Oh no. I shouldn't have said that. And I couldn't take it back.

Wat the weasel (and the other animals) were probably not failures at all. Only the Boy and I were. I failed on my quest to bring my family back together like we used to be, and the Boy failed in taking me to my destiny. I hadn't changed back. Maybe I never would.

Wat looked away, uncomfortable and hurt. The Boy's eyes held such regret and sadness.

"I'm sorry. I didn't mean the last part. Truly," I said. The Boy's and Wat's eyes softened. "But we have to help them."

"I don't know what to do, Albie," the Boy said.

Neither did I. But I wouldn't give up. Maybe Caragh or Rory would help me, if only I could get to them privately— away from Bronagh. But first I needed to check Mum's journals.

We waited as the howling quieted. When it was good and dark, I scampered around the back of the house, leaving the Boy and Wat looking dumbfounded in the moonlight.

The faerie window was still open a crack. Leaping onto the ledge, I slipped through and silently launched to the floor and raced up to my parents' room.

There was a big lump under the white bedspread that could only mean one thing. The hag must have chosen a different bed after I'd dirtied the one in my room.

How dare she sleep in my parents' bed!

Not being able to help myself, I climbed up and stood on her chest, my face in her own. It's a terrifying thing, at least I hoped it would be, to wake up and find a furry face staring right at you, not six inches away.

She breathed with her mouth open, snoring slightly. Her skin was flabby, like there was too much of it draping over her skull, puddling in wrinkles near her ears. Remembering my task, I glanced over at the bookshelf, my rabbit eyes quickly adjusting to the darkness. None of my mother's journals sat at the top. They were gone. All of her books were gone. The only thing remaining was a framed quote from someone named Daniel Webster my mother had kept near her desk.

"There is nothing so powerful as truth—and often nothing so strange."

These were the only words my mother had for me.

Frustrated, I let my whiskers tickle the hag's cheek and was rewarded with a startled scream.

"Get out of my house!" I hissed at her face.

She leaped up, causing me to fall off the bed altogether.

"Never!" she squawked. "And there's nothing you can do about it, rabbit. No, this is *my* place now. And the girls— their souls will be mine, and soon. I've kept watch. Oh, yes, I knew when I was forced to send you on that ratty boat you'd eventually come back to Cork and old Bronagh. It's even better than I hoped—except that *you* are still a dirty hare. Can't take a rabbit's soul, now can I? Rabbits don't even have souls!"

I knew that was a lie. I was a girl who was a rabbit—still me. Albie.

"I know what you are," I said, using the only weapon I had: the truth. "I know you are a sluagh."

"Been getting educated, I see. Well then, you'll know that

- 224 -

getting rid of me ain't no easy task. But you, on the other hand, you'll be gone before sunrise."

Caragh and Rory rushed in.

"What's going on? Why are you in *here*, Miss Bronagh? What did you do this time, Albie?" Caragh, hands on her hips, was reasserting herself as the one in charge.

"That unclean beastie ruined the bed in the other room. I had to find a different place to sleep. Oh, my poor old bones," Bronagh said, faking distress. "I told you there was something off about this hare. It claims to be your relation, but if that was true, why did it threaten me? Me, a harmless old woman! I've done nothing but help!" Bronagh began crying big fake tears.

I rolled my eyes, not that anyone could see, since the room was still dark.

Rory found the lamp and turned it on.

Bronagh was sobbing, most pitifully. Her sadness seeped through the room, and I watched as it touched everyone. My sisters' eyes filled with pity.

This was some powerful magic.

"Come now," Caragh said, putting a comforting arm around the old beast. "You've got yourself all riled up."

Bronagh pointed her bony finger at me. "This creature must be banished from this house."

"You're right," said a voice behind me. It was Rory. There were dark circles under her eyes, giving her a frightening look. I could well believe she had scared off a bunch of sheep. "All unnecessary creatures must be banished from this house."

"Yes!" Bronagh cried. "The impostor must be banished.

And even if it was your sister, which it is *not*, but even if it was, how can you forgive her for what she did? She changed you, all of you. She stole years from your lives!"

Even if I couldn't hear it very well, I could feel the vibrations. The Howler was there, with me. There was no escaping it.

In trancelike voices, my sisters began chanting in unison. "She must go. She must go."

I'd be lying if I said I wasn't both terrified and heartbroken. I wanted to run out of that room out into the forest, find the Boy, and have him take me away from here and go—

Where?

Where exactly did I think I was going to go?

There was no place else left for me.

"She must go. She must go."

No!

I would stay and fight this thing.

"All unnecessary creatures must go," said Rory again.

"Now wait just a minute, Rory—" I began, trying to lift my small rabbit voice over the dueling sounds of the chanting and the howling. But was stopped by two things.

The first was a familiar glint in Rory's eye, the kind she'd get when we played a game together and she'd just thought of the perfect way to win.

The second was the way she turned slightly from me, just the teeniest bit, and shifted her gaze toward the hideous Bronagh. "Which is why we are banishing *you*, Bronagh, from this house."

"Me? You can't!" she squawked.

"Oh, but we can," Rory said, ice in her voice. And confidence. She turned to me and whispered, "We gave her chamomile tea, hoping she'd fall asleep so we could find you." Then she turned and glared at the hag.

Bronagh drew herself up, much taller than anyone else in the room. She pointed at me. "She's evil! Think about what she did to all of you! Turning you into rabbits! Yes, I know the truth!"

"I forgave her for that a long time ago," said Rory.

There is nothing so powerful as truth.

"You did?" I whispered, wilting a little.

The howling quieted a little, too.

"Of course I did. Turning into a rabbit was the best thing that ever happened to me," Rory said.

Caragh continued the chant.

"She must go! She must go!"

Rory and Caragh gathered around me. Their voices had changed; no longer were they trancelike or under some sort of spell.

Bronagh cackled. She was too wrapped up in her own vileness to notice something as simple and sweet as sisterly love.

"Rory, what are we going to do?" I cried.

Caragh grabbed me and held me to her chest. "I forgave you, too."

Nothing so powerful.

"It's not Albie who must go, but you," said Rory. They turned and faced the sluagh. "We forgive Albie."

The howling died completely. There was nothing left of it at all.

"Bronagh, you are banished from this house!" Caragh cried, pointing her finger at the beastly creature.

There was a cackling cry.

The sluagh burst into a flock of white birds that flew out the window and into the night.

And in the arms of my sisters, I turned into a girl again.

Part III

IN WHICH IT ENDS
WHERE IT BEGINS

Chapter Twenty-Four

How long had it been since I'd seen the shores of Hybrasil? Weeks? Months? I'd lost all perspective.

However, spending several days on a small boat helped me find it again. Now that I was a girl, I couldn't talk to the Sea in the same way anymore. She no longer gave me her verses to ponder. I tried so hard to listen for them, but now . . .

It was just me, Albie, against the world.

Oh, and the Boy.

He'd been quite surprised to see me in my girl form. He wasn't the only one. I cried when I looked in the mirror for the first time. Caragh said she did, too.

"Don't worry, Albie honey, you'll get used to yourself again."

"But I barely look like me." My hair was longer, and so was my nose. And the freckles that had dusted my cheek were nearly gone.

"It's been two years since you've seen yourself. You've grown up a bit."

Rory hugged me. "I missed my rabbit-self, too. But you're meant to be a girl."

I hugged her back.

That's what those first few days after we'd banished Bronagh were like. Lots of hugs and sister talk. "How did you know?" I'd asked them. "When did you figure out that Bronagh meant us harm?" I didn't want to make a big deal out the fact that she'd obviously bewitched them and that they almost let her get rid of me, but I was curious.

"I'm not quite sure," said Caragh.

"Perhaps the three of us together were just too much for the old bat," Rory said, smiling. "I like to think that love is always the strongest thing."

Caragh and Rory let me choose from their old clothes, since mine no longer fit.

As much as I wanted to stay, I still had a job to do. A job that required the Boy.

"You're not how I pictured you," he said as I made my way to the dock where he'd anchored his boat. He hadn't been up to the house since we banished Bronagh, claiming he had repairs to make on his boat. I think he just felt awkward.

I was in a flowered dress that was far too fancy for traveling in a boat across the Sea. But it was Caragh's, and she knew how I'd always wanted it. Rory gave me her blue sweater, which didn't match but was almost as soft as my fur had been.

"What did you imagine?" I asked, a bit peeved.

"I don't know. I thought you'd look fiercer."

"Looks can be deceiving," I replied.

"Obviously."

What did *fierce* look like, after all? Were my eyes supposed to shoot out lightning when I glared? Was my hair (which Caragh had braided, since it was quite matted) supposed to catch fire when I got angry? Seriously.

So if you are wondering if the trip across the ocean was awkward between me and the Boy, it was.

"It's different now, isn't it?" the Boy said as we rowed ashore on Hybrasil. I didn't respond. I hadn't even wanted him to come. It would have been better for him to stay back with Caragh. He could have helped her in the Cork house. But he wouldn't loan me the boat.

"There's no beach at all. Look, the garden's underwater, too," he continued.

Alas, the garden! The beautiful vegetables. I mourned them for a moment, even the cabbages, though I couldn't explain why. They were just plants, after all. But still, an empty hole was growing inside of me.

We rowed past the drawbridge in the pebbly shallows. The Boy climbed out and offered me his hand. I was still getting used to being human again. I had the urge to scamper off, up to the castle, which no longer looked so large, but I could only walk on my two, not-so-sturdy, legs.

There was no movement anywhere near the castle.

Maybe the Magician was napping.

"I want to go to the other side." The words tripped from my lips even before I thought about them.

"We might not be able to get there. The stick bridge might already be underwater. Actually, we're lucky the whole island isn't completely submerged," the Boy said.

I looked up to see the castle's tall, crumbling tower, but I wasn't ready to go in, afraid of what we might find.

"I can swim across if the stick bridge is gone. It was a worthless bridge anyway." I was walking, sometimes wading, through what was left of the grounds.

"Don't you want to check on him first? Let him know that we are here?"

I pretended that I didn't hear. It wasn't that I didn't want to see the Magician. I did desperately. But what if . . . what if he wasn't . . .

There are things you can't let yourself say sometimes, and they are so awful, you can't let yourself even think them. But they are there, hiding noisily in the back of your brain.

Oh, so noisily hiding.

The bridge was wrecked. Maybe from the wind, although if I didn't know better, I would swear that a wave from the ocean came far inland to swoop in and break it. Like maybe the Sea didn't want me or anyone else to go across anymore. But I was small, and there was enough wreckage left for me to find my way.

If the bridge was this bad, I couldn't help but wonder about the other side. What had happened since I was last there?

The wind began to kick up.

Thankfully, there was no howling. I hadn't heard any howling since Cork—since I'd turned back into a girl. Perhaps it was just something that rabbits heard.

Except that the Boy had heard it, too. And Caragh and Rory, too.

Maybe the mystery of the Howler was something I would never solve.

It wasn't hard to navigate across the decrepit bridge before, one paw here, another there. Even now, using feet and hands instead of paws, I was still remarkably nimble. At least I had that.

Balance your weight. Balance. Balance.

It was even windier. You'd think that in the wind, a howl would feel right at home. But still, no howling. I got to the other side.

Finally gone.

I was surprised. If there's one thing I learned, it was that bad things rarely faded permanently. They had a tendency to come back again.

And so, too, did good things. Sometimes. So I closed my eyes and hoped with all my might, but when I opened them, he wasn't there.

My father, I mean. I knew he wouldn't be, of course. Perhaps the Boy was right and he'd never really been there at all. Papa thought he'd dreamed *me*, but maybe I had dreamed *him*. I could picture him, holding the medal he hadn't yet won and giving it an odd look. I could still feel the touch of his hand on my rabbit back.

But I was alone now. Just me and the wind.

The small shack where I had cast the spell was now in ruins. It looked like a hundred years had passed since I'd last seen it, but I knew that was impossible.

"Time moves differently here, Albie. Of course, you remember that, don't you?"

Though his voice was weak and papery, no longer deep and gravelly, I would recognize it anywhere.

The Magician sat on what was left of the back porch, in a rickety old rocking chair. His white hair was nearly gone. He was so wrinkled, it was difficult to find his eyes in his face.

But it was him. Of course it was.

"You've found your destiny and changed back into a girl, I see. Though would it be wrong of me to say that I liked your rabbit-self equally well?"

I wanted to throw myself into his arms, the arms of my grandfather, but instead I asked awkwardly, "Why are you here?"

"Why are any of us here?" he answered.

"I mean *here*, on this side of the island?"

His beard was shorter than last I saw it, trimmed nicely, too, as if he was getting ready for something important.

"Thought it was about time."

Silence hung in the air between us, thin and fragile. I knew we'd have to break it, that we'd have to talk, to say things that maybe neither of us wanted to hear. I didn't want to continue.

The Magician sighed. He didn't want to continue, either.

I decided evasion was better than confrontation, at least at this moment. "Why are you dressed up all fancy? I've never seen you like this."

"I used to dress up and trim my beard all the time. See this suit? It's my fancy-go-to-a-meeting suit."

It looked just like a regular old suit—kind of faded and frayed. In the lapel he had pinned a rather sad flower that drooped to the right, except when the Magician spoke, then it jostled back and forth in rhythm with his words.

"And who are you going to meet?"

"Why, you, Albie. Of course it's you."

He couldn't have known. I only just decided a few moments ago to come here.

"And who else?" I asked, but he didn't say anything. He just looked at his wrist for a watch that wasn't there and muttered something about it "getting late" and that he had "much to do."

"Well, no one here is stopping you. Go ahead and do whatever it was you were going to do." The words came out more harshly than I intended, so I tried to make myself look busy, which is hard when you're doing nothing. I went into the ramshackle house and started to look through things. Eventually, I found my way to the table and just sat there. I didn't mean to be so mean. This wasn't what I expected. The Magician was acting like he was ready to die, and now that I was finally here and supposed to save him, I really didn't know what to do.

The Magician walked very slowly and noisily into the shack, with the aid of his cane.

"You'd best be on your way, Albie, though I'd be lying if I said that I'm not glad to see you one last time."

"I'm—I'm glad to see you, too. But it's not for the last time. I'm sorry I couldn't save Hybrasil, but I came back for you. I came back to bring you home with me."

"But I am home."

"If you stay, your home will soon be at the bottom of the Sea."

"Would that be so bad?"

There was a breeze, and it was strangely warm. The grasses waved, green and vibrant. Did they know they would soon be covered by ocean?

"Yes! It would be pretty awful."

"Well, Albie, that's because you don't know everything."

"I know a lot more than you think. I've learned a lot in my adventures. More than you can imagine."

The ground moved, causing my chair to wobble. Then it shifted some more, knocking the Magician to the ground.

"It's happening! It's happening! You must go now, Albie!" he cried. I ran toward him, falling twice as a deep rumble began beneath us.

"I won't leave you here!"

I tried to help him up, but even though he looked frail and small, he was too heavy for me.

"It's not your choice to make."

"Well, maybe it is," I said. I tried again, and this time, miraculously, I propped him up and forced him to walk. "We're going to Cork, to your family. The Boy is taking us in his boat. We just have to get to him."

And then, like the earth itself was cracking, a horrible cry came from its cavernous depths. The wind reared up like an angry horse whipping its mane. Just as we made our way through the doorway, the shack collapsed upon itself and was sucked down below into a swirling whirlpool.

I was too late. I'd spent too long searching for my own destiny, and I'd lost my chance to save him—to save the old man who had once saved me and my sisters. My grandfather.

And now I had doomed him. And me.

"Aaaaaaaooooowwwwwwww!"

"What is that sound? Is that your Howler, Albie?" called the Magician over the ruckus.

The hole was swallowing up more and more of the island, when a new sound joined the Howler. It was the sound of my own screams.

"Boy!" I cried, and the water sloshed against my knees.

"BOY!" I cried again when a wave knocked me over and the water closed over my head for a moment. I knew he couldn't hear me—he hadn't crossed the stick bridge with me. He was much too far away.

My ears rang with a menacing cackle. It couldn't be, but it was.

Bronagh.

The last time I tried to call for the Boy, my mouth filled with water, and I sank. Down, down, and farther down.

Chapter Twenty-Five

"Albie?"

When I opened my eyes underwater, they burned and stung. I could see nothing.

All I ever wanted was to have my parents back again, living in our house with my sisters. That's all.

But time has a way of changing things.

In this moment, all I wanted was to breathe.

"Albie, remember the last time . . ."

Her voice was a whisper in the water. But yes, as I plummeted to the bottom of the Sea, I did remember the last time I was deep in the ocean. It was when I met Barinthus and swam to an underwater cavern where I could breathe. But I'd had the magical bridle then. Now it was just me.

"Remember!" the Sea commanded.

Was there a cave under Hybrasil? (Or what used to be Hybrasil.)

I swam deeper, searching frantically for an opening, but I was down so far below the surface, it was too dark to see.

Under the ocean's surface it's quiet, so quiet. I wanted to call out to the Sea, but a person can only make glugging noises underwater. Besides, she knew I was there.

Down I sank. I didn't fight it.

Something grabbed my hand and pulled me under a slippery, algae-covered formation of rocks, then upward until my face broke through the surface. Air, even air salty with spray, tastes so good. Coughing even felt good.

The Boy pushed me up onto the edge of the small hole, then climbed out of it behind me. He bent over with his face close to my own. "Are you okay, Albie? Can you hear me?"

Still coughing, I nodded. "The Magician? Where is he?"

The Boy shrugged. "I'm not sure. I didn't see him. I heard you calling, and I came."

"How did you hear me? You were on the other side of the island."

"There's a lot you don't know about me, Albie."

The cavern was different from the one I'd been in earlier.

This was much smaller and with no fancy furniture to make it feel cozy. This was cold and dark like the inside of a hole.

And it was filled with air. Glorious air. Like some sort of strange, underwater bubble.

"Where are we?" I asked.

"This cave is . . . well . . . it's mine."

"It has air!"

"You can thank my father for that."

I took in its emptiness. "This is where you live?"

"Not most of the time. I spend most of my time hauling rabbits across the Sea. But this place is my own."

"Why don't you live with your father?" I asked.

"Same reason you don't live with yours. It's not really possible."

"Oh," I said, pretending to know what he meant.

"Barinthus doesn't need a son. He just needs someone to take over eventually. So I guess that would be me. But he'll be at it for another millennium most likely. Plenty of time for me to learn what to do."

"So," I said.

"So."

The awkwardness in the cave was replaced with the realization of the situation at hand. We had to save the Magician—and the Howler was still out there somewhere.

"The Magician? Is he . . . ," he began.

"I think Bronagh has him. I heard her laughing. And I heard the Howler, too," I finished.

"The Howler doesn't matter. Not now. Not with the Magician taken by the sluagh."

This would be her final act of revenge upon me. I had deprived her of my sisters' souls. So she had come to take the Magician's.

What a cruel end for him! He'd been planning to sink into the ocean, his beloved Murien, and simply cease to be. That much was obvious. I'd been too late to save his life, and now I'd ruined his death, too.

"What will she do to him?" I asked.

"Torture his soul, most likely. What did you think? Take him to tea?"

I was tempted to lash out, but I knew that wouldn't get us anywhere. I took a deep breath and asked as calmly as I could, "Where will she have taken him?"

The Boy was quiet. He kicked a small shell against the wall of the cave that came rolling back to his foot. "I have no idea."

A wave splashed up through a hole in the floor. Foamy bubbles surrounded our feet. The Boy kicked at the bubbles in the same frustrated way that he had kicked at the shell.

Until I stopped him.

"Shhh," I said. "Can't you hear it?"

"I can only hear the sound of foam bubbles popping."

But I could hear more. Much more.

In each foam bubble was a message from the Sea. And as it popped, the words traveled into my brain.

It was strange, listening to the Sea as a person rather than as a rabbit. My rabbit ears were much better. But my girl-heart, why, it understood things that ears by themselves cannot.

The Sea was weeping.

> *"Oh, Albie, my sweet,*
> *It is too late.*
> *Even I cannot save*
> *Him from a terrible fate."*

I had never known the Sea to give up. Not once.

She sobbed some more, softly as ever, as the last of the foam bubbles vanished.

I eyed the water as it lapped against the rocky floor. The Boy followed my gaze and reached into his pocket, revealing the golden kelpie bridle.

"I know, I know, there aren't any kelpies around here. But it's enchanted, and it might help you. It certainly can't hurt."

He handed me the bridle, which I slipped into the waistband of my soggy dress to keep safe.

I realized then that he wasn't planning to go with me.

I guess I'd been hoping that he'd have a plan. But in the end, despite being the son of Death's Ferryman, he was still only a boy.

A boy with no idea what to do.

"It's your destiny, Albie," he said at last.

I held my breath as I jumped into the hole. Then I began swimming as if my life depended on it.

Because it did.

But not only my life. The Magician's as well. And quite possibly the Boy's life, too.

Down, down, into the blackest part of the Sea I swam until I thought my lungs would burst from my chest. Below the shadow of the underwater rocks of the Boy's cave I swam, until my legs ached from kicking. When I passed the rocks that supported Hybrasil, I swam, up, up, up to the small circle of light that could only be the sun.

When I broke through the surface, gasping and coughing, every muscle in my body burning, I could see what remained of Hybrasil. Two small peaks that had once been tall hills were now separated by a thick river of ocean. Rocky, craggy beaches surrounded each peak. White birds darted in and around each peak.

No castle. No stick bridge. No shack.

And no sign of the Magician on what was now the new beach. No sign of life at all except for those birds.

The Sea carried me ever so gently to the shore of one of the peaks. I was glad I didn't have to give much effort, for I'd never felt so exhausted in my life. My limbs were noodly and heavy, and I still felt like there wasn't enough air in the world for me to inhale. But I had to go on.

The Sea deposited me onto the pebbles of a ledge, along with thousands of bits of white shell. Not the smooth kind, where the edges are polished and even, but freshly broken, sharp and jagged.

I wanted to call out for the Magician, when I realized that I didn't even know his real name. So I called out the other name I knew him by, this one sounding strange as it tumbled for the first time from my human lips.

"Grandfather?"

I was timid at first, but then I yelled until my throat, raw from the salt water, turned hoarse and raspy.

"Grandfather! Grandfather! Are you here? Where are you?"

I whipped around, taking in what was left of Hybrasil. He had to be somewhere, didn't he?

A large wave knocked me to the ground. Now wasn't the time for a message from the Sea, but it was impossible to ignore her.

"Albie!"

Her voice, a whisper on the wind, came from the east. When I turned, that's when I saw him.

The Sea had floated my grandfather to the edge of the Boy's empty boat. He struggled to hoist himself over but eventually made it. Lifting an oar, he shakily dipped it into the water and began rowing.

The sluagh didn't have him at all. He had escaped to the Sea.

And it was my destiny to let him go.

Still, I called for him.

"Grandfather!"

I might have seen him wave at me, but he was too far away to tell.

So that was it. He was sailing out on his beloved Sea, and that would be the end.

"Goodbye, Grandfather."

Chapter Twenty-Six

But it wasn't the end of the Magician. Not yet. It might have been the end he deserved—but what we deserve is not always what we get. My parents deserved better than what they got, but that's war for you. Everyone who's been killed by war probably deserved better.

As if summoned by my calls, the birds that darted among what was left of Hybrasil now changed their target. These were the very same birds Bronagh had transformed into when we banished her from Cork. They headed straight for the Magician.

And they attacked.

The sluagh birds went after the Magician like seagulls fighting over a crust of bread on the beach. The squawking and screeching. The flapping and crashing into each other—as if there wasn't enough of the Magician's soul to go around. I expected him to bat them away with his arms, but he simply sat in the boat and let them attack. Despite the fact that he'd never hear me over the sound of the howling, I tried again.

"Grandfather!"

I thought I was going to throw up as I watched those horrible birds tear off little bits and pieces of his fine black suit. But I calmed myself. That's not quite true. The Sea calmed me. Soft as an evening breeze, she washed over my feet and ankles, leaving treasures at my feet: more broken shards of shell.

And in the sky, out past the flock of evil birds, clouds in the shape of a flying ship drifted past.

"Albie," the wind called again. But it wasn't the wind nor was it the Sea. Not really. It sounded more like Isolde. *"Be brave,"* said the Isolde wind.

The *Brave Paddy* was part fog, part mist, part who even knows. But it was there, and her words were stronger than any howler.

"Courage!"

I quickly gathered up the shells at my feet, most of them sharp and misshapen, and stuffed them into my pockets. The golden bridle burned against my waist as I pulled it out.

I knew what I had to do.

I waded out into the Sea and dipped the bridle into the

ocean. The Boy had said that the kelpies were far from here, but if Isolde's ship could travel across time as a cloud, then maybe I could summon a kelpie to come when I wanted it to. Hybrasil was enchanted, after all.

And when you are friends with the Sea (and she is your grandmother), then she just might be able to lend a hand . . . or a wave.

"Please, please help me . . . Grandmother Murien," I whispered. "Bring me a kelpie so I can save the Magician."

> *"Oh, Albie. You call me by a name*
> *I've not heard for a long, long time.*
> *I am not sure that I am even Murien*
> *anymore.*
> *Once upon a time, perhaps . . .*
> *but no more."*

And as she sighed, a big wave crashed against me, drenching me with stinging spray.

"Please!"

> *"It will be dangerous.*
> *But then, you have never run*
> *from danger,*
> *have you, my little rabbit girl?"*

I dangled the bridle into the ocean once again. The ocean sent more sharp shells, creating tiny cuts along my knees and legs, which bled freely into the gray-blue water.

"That is all I can do
The rest is up to you."

The kelpie was golden green and his mane streamed behind him like liquid copper. It mingled with my blood, and I knew then the reason that the Sea had cut me—to attract the leader of the herd. But he didn't bite—despite how tempted he might be. The golden bridle prevented that. I slipped it over his face and climbed on his back, all the while the howling continued in the distance.

The wind called, *"Be careful."*

But I couldn't tell, was it Isolde or the Sea?

Or both.

I didn't need to tell the kelpie where I wanted to go, or try to steer him. We raced across the waves to the Boy's boat.

The Magician was bleeding and raggedy but still alive. He didn't even try to protect himself from the birds. And they were vicious. Somehow I'd led the sluagh straight to him.

The Howler shrieked louder than the screeches of the sluagh birds.

"Stop!" I cried, as if that would do any good.

"I banished you back in Cork!" I cried.

The birds laughed. Or squawked so loud that I couldn't even hear the howling or the Sea.

"My sisters forgave me!" I yelled. "They forgave me!"

Isolde's cloud ship came into view, and I just might have heard her say, *"But you never forgave yourself. She feeds on your grief and your guilt."*

I felt in my pocket for the shell shards and yanked the bridle off the kelpie.

"Keep still!" I commanded the water beast beneath my legs. And he did.

Balancing my weight as best as I could and using the bridle as a slingshot, I flung a piece of shell at one of the birds.

I missed as the birds mocked me with their calls, the howls swirling their taunts around me.

I took aim with another shell and missed again.

You never forgave yourself.

Could I do it now? Could I forgive myself? My sisters had forgiven me; they had found grace. They didn't hold my mistake against me.

I reached for another shell, this one stabbing my finger as I pulled it into position. I took aim, but before I let go, I thought deep down in my brain, in my heart, and in my soul and whispered, *"I forgive you, Albie. I forgive . . . myself."*

The shell was sharp as a razor and sliced through the bird, which vanished from the sky with a haggard cry, leaving only a small shower of feathers to rain down upon the Magician.

The Howler quieted, just a bit, but it was enough.

I took aim at all the remaining birds, either minions of Bronagh or bits of the old witch herself, I wasn't sure. I didn't know how that sort of magic worked. I only know that with every shell that hit a bird, the howling got quieter. Every time I forgave myself, the Howler got quieter still. So I shot them all from the sky.

Shell by shell.

Bird by bird.

They disappeared like snow into the Sea.

All except one, perched on the Magician's shoulder like a pirate's parrot, preening its wings.

"Go ahead, *little sister*, sling your shell at me." Bronagh's voice came from the evil beak. "You could miss and hit him dead between the eyes. Or maybe right in his eye. Go ahead. Let's see how lucky you are. Perhaps your aim is better than your spell casting. It could hardly be worse!"

I reached into my pocket for another shell. But there were none left.

Waves splashed against the kelpie and me, and I was poked by something sharp.

I glanced down to see something shiny floating magically in the water by my leg. Impossibly floating.

Not a shell at all.

My father's bronze cross medal.

The medal was poised in my hand, and I took aim, though my eyes burned with tears I refused to shed. The Magician's eyes were closed. Whether he was trying to hide his fear or resigning himself to his fate, I couldn't tell.

"You're afraid, aren't you?" Bronagh said. "Afraid you'll miss me. Afraid you'll never have your sisters again. Afraid of your destiny. You're a fool and a coward, Alberta O'Brien."

Well, she was half-right. I might have been a fool—but I was no coward.

I let go of the medal, saying a prayer for my grandparents, for my mother and father, and for myself, the poor rabbit girl who had punished herself long enough. The bronze blade soared through the air, finding its mark in the heart of the wicked bird.

The howling faded to a hiss, then into nothing at all.

The Magician opened his eyes.

A rush of water lifted the kelpie and me up over a wave that found its way to the Boy's boat and the Magician.

"Look!" the Boy cried.

I turned around to see the tip of the mountains of Hybrasil sinking into the Sea with a deep sucking noise.

The Magician closed his eyes and placed his hands over his heart.

The kelpie nudged my leg with his nose a couple of times, obviously wanting me to get off his back. So I did. He didn't even try to eat me as I gracelessly dumped myself onto the hard floorboards of the boat.

Something sharp poked my back as I tried to sit up. As I felt for it, my hand recognized the pointy edges, and I clasped it tightly. So shiny and bright, exactly what courage would look like if you could see it. The Brave Captain Paddy O'Brien's Victoria Cross medal.

I kissed it.

The Magician took it and pinned it to the front of my sweater.

"Stubborn and brave. An excellent combination in a rabbit girl, don't you think?" he said.

I might have wiped my nose with the back of my sleeve. Then something thumped the boat, and I turned quickly. "Here," I said to the kelpie, holding the bridle in front of his mouth so he could grab it if he chose. "Thank you for your help. No one ever need control you again."

He seemed confused, so I dropped the bridle with a plunk into the Sea. "It's yours if you want it."

Like a puppy chasing a ball, the golden-green kelpie sank under the water until I could see only wisps of the copper mane, writhing down into the deep. Then nothing but foam.

"Now, why did you have to go and do that? What am I going to tell him?" The familiar voice was more annoyed than angry. Whipping around, I found the Boy pulled up next to us on a long, narrow, very grand ferryboat. On both ends were ornate carvings of sea serpents.

"Your father's boat?"

"Yes."

"Stolen?"

"Borrowed."

"Of course."

The Magician sighed heavily. "It's time, then, isn't it? I'll go quietly. Just make sure Albie gets out of here all right."

He rose, preparing to leave the rowboat and step onto the death ferry, nearly tipping us over in the process. Not that he would have minded. He'd have landed in the Sea. But perhaps she wasn't ready for him yet, for the waves beneath us calmed suddenly and completely, and we didn't tip.

"Not so fast," said the Boy with a smirk so small, a regular person wouldn't have even noticed it at all. But a girl who spent a great deal of her life as a rabbit would.

"I've been checking Barinthus's list, and it is true, you are on it. Mr. A. MacConmara."

The Magician let out a slow sigh. "Yes. I know. Let's get on with it."

"You know, it's not really *your* decision when to die. That decision belongs to Death and Death alone. So you must be like everyone else and live every day like it is important, because it is. You've spent so much of your life in hiding—is that living?"

The Magician's eyes became huge as he looked at the Boy, whose smirk was no longer tiny; instead it was a full-fledged, sneaky smile.

"Now, according to the scroll, you've some time yet," said the Boy. "Use it wisely."

"What? How?" the Magician asked.

"You've kept your secrets, my friend, and I'll keep mine."

The Boy waved his long oar over his rowboat as if he were the Magician and the oar were his wand. The smaller boat began rowing itself away from the ferry. "I'm guessing you know where you want to go, don't you, Albie?" he asked.

I smiled at the Boy.

Yes. I knew.

"Come, Grandfather. I'm taking you home."

Chapter Twenty-Seven

We missed Rory's Christmas celebration by a month—for the Boy still had difficulties navigating time and space perfectly, but it didn't really matter.

It felt like Christmas because we were home. All of us. Isolde, too, but just for a quick visit. She anchored the *Brave Paddy* behind a cloud and swung down her rope ladder for hugs and tea.

Around the kitchen table, amid mugs of hot Earl Grey and freshly baked carrot scones (we all still had a love of carrots), I told my sisters the truth about the old man on Hybrasil who had taken us in.

My sisters were shocked, of course, to discover the truth of their grandparents. And then, in less than a minute, they weren't shocked at all. When you hear the truth and feel it and know it's real, everything else falls into place. True, not many

girls could claim an ancient Magician (who had lived more years than most people can count) as a grandfather, and the Sea (who once walked the land as a woman named Murien) as their grandmother, but then again, not many girls spent time as rabbits on the hidden island of Hybrasil.

It took hard work to make the place feel like our home again. (And for us to behave like a family of humans.) The Boy stayed around for a while to help. He liked being noticed, I think, and not fading into the background. (And Caragh certainly noticed him.) Rory thought we needed plants in pots inside the house. She had gotten used to living among the greenery on Hybrasil. And so we worked at making the living room into a garden room. Caragh thought we needed a schedule of chores so that everyone felt included and needed, because everyone was. And she didn't want things falling to pieces when she went back to cannonballing when her circus finally moved to Cork. I didn't like the chore schedule much, but she was the oldest . . . sort of. We had a grandfather now. We agreed to fix up our parents' room for him, making it far more cozy than that drafty old castle.

He still had trouble answering when we referred to him as Grandfather.

"Please forgive me," he would say. "My ears are old and not used to hearing such a glorious word in reference to myself."

"What should we call you, then?" I finally asked. "We can't go around referring to you as the Magician, now, can we? And it's not like we know your real name."

"It's Albert," he said, looking me straight in the eye with pride, and a touch of sadness.

I'd been named for him and hadn't even known it.

※ ※ ※

And then it was summer.

Summer in Cork is especially magical. The meadows are

green and the sky and Sea compete to see who can be the most blue. (The Sea wins most of the time. Of course she does.)

Grandfather's garden was coming up lush and vibrant— even more so than the garden on Hybrasil. Rory was helping him to care for it. He complained occasionally that he'd like to have his journals back, he'd kept good records on gardening, but all the Magician's books went down with his library on Hybrasil. Hundreds of books now rested at the bottom of the Sea. I liked to picture the Sea reading some of the tales to the turtles or dolphins—not that they'd be much interested in sitting around and listening to stories. That's unique to humans, I think.

And rabbit girls.

Caragh and the Boy—well, we all saw that one coming, didn't we? He came around on his boat whenever the seasons changed and did all sorts of things to impress Caragh, like pushing up his sleeves when he rowed so she could see his muscles. It was ridiculous and it made me laugh. But I did hope they would find a way to be together. Perhaps it wasn't possible, with him being the son of Barinthus, and Caragh being, well, Caragh. But she was no ordinary girl, and not just because she spent a lot of time as a rabbit.

Isolde continued to visit from time to time, always bringing treats and gossip from Nodnol. There was a new kind of curse the pirates were using in battle that could turn you into a newt! Luckily, Isolde told us, she was too crafty and stealthy with her ship to have been hit with it. I asked her about her "crafty and stealth" appearance in the clouds on the day I had faced the sluagh as Hybrasil sank into the ocean. She said, "Why, Albie, I have no idea what you are talking about."

Liar.

But I've told my share of lies, and I'll not hold it against her. It proves she still uses her magic a little, and I think our mother would be proud.

As for Rory, each week she cooked a Sunday dinner of vegetable soup, homemade bread, colcannon, and chocolate crème cakes. It was the kind of meal that warmed your heart as well as your stomach. Bann and Hecate usually dropped by for a nibble or two. They had long conversations with Rory, though none of the rest of us had any idea what they were saying. (Not surprisingly, only the Boy and the Magician ate the colcannon. Yuck.)

Actually, we all had a bit of magic from Mum. I hadn't thought of it earlier, but each of us had a special talent. Caragh could make herself invisible. Isolde could be in two places at once. In addition to talking to animals, Rory always knew how to give her sisters the compassion that they needed in any moment. Perhaps that is the best kind of magic.

My sisters were special indeed.

My mother knew it. We found the other half of the letter Mum had written to the Magician, back when she'd sent us to Hybrasil. Bronagh had tried to destroy it, but we found it stuffed in Mum's books, which Bronagh had hidden in the attic.

> Dear Father,
>
> I hope this letter finds you well, for with it comes very precious cargo. Each of my daughters, Caragh, Isolde, Rory, and Albie, possesses unique gifts. It is possible with proper tutelage at the right time, the older three might be able to develop their gifts. Or they might not. It is difficult to predict. This is not the case with Albie. Already her abilities are apparent, and potentially dangerous to herself and others. Her passionate nature married with her unbridled talent should not go unwatched. I hope to be able to retrieve my girls someday, but the reality is that it may already be too late for me. Thus, it is with a heavy heart that

The rest of it was torn off. That was the part that Bronagh let him have:

> I am sending my children into your care. Look after them.
>
> Your daughter

Grandfather pretended not to cry when we read it.

So yes, I'm going to be very careful with magic. Somehow, I'd plucked a vision of my father across space and time, across the very threshold of death, with only a rusted hero's medal, not to mention the whole turning-my-sisters-into-rabbits thing. But nothing helped me to bring my mother back.

Instead, my grief and guilt created a monster.

The Boy explained it best when he told me about the nature of magic. "Feelings are powerful things, Albie, the most powerful things, actually. Why else would you risk your own future to bring everyone together? Feelings. How else could you have made the Howler? Yes, it was your creation. That's why you could never outrun it. It was the strength of your emotions. And how did you defeat the sluagh and save the Magician? Feelings. The ability to feel something so strongly as to change *everything*, well, that is no different from spells and incantations, really. What is magic but one way of doing things? That's the truth of it."

There is nothing so powerful as truth, and often nothing so strange.

I'd be careful if I was going to dabble in magic again. Who knew what magic I was really capable of? If I were to guess, I would say that I inherited something unbelievably powerful, yet possibly sort of deadly. I was the best and worst of the lot of us. Mum wasn't here to teach me properly, and though I could ask the Magician, I'd rather spend the time we had left together doing other things. Simple things. The kind of things you might write poems about and read to someone on a summer's day.

> *Sometimes we lose things and we are broken.*
> *Sometimes we find things,*
> *and sometimes,*
> *if we are lucky,*
> *we mend.*

I'd find magic again. When the time was right, I'd learn the proper way to do things. Of course I would.

From my window, I could see the Sea. And I was sure that my grandmother could see me as well. She waved to me, and I knew it was time to go and listen to her poetry.

I hear her now and then. I'm the only one, though. Even the Magician can no longer listen to her poems.

So I write down the poems from the Sea and read them to him each night. Sometimes we walk slowly together to the beach. It's quite a ways from the house, and it tires him greatly, but he doesn't care. He likes to roll his pants up and feel the cold rush of water on his feet. It's as close to frolicking as he gets.

The war wages on out in the world. It may seem as if we forget what horrors continue outside our little corner of the world. But the truth is, we will never forget. The war took Mum and Papa. They weren't content to sit idly by and allow the progress of evil. I don't know if their sacrifice was worth it in the end, though. But that's the thing, isn't it? In the moment you never know if what you are attempting will work.

We can only try.

✳ ✳ ✳

Sometimes the Boy and Caragh are there when we walk to the beach, working on the Boy's boat, which is magical and doesn't really need any work. When they see us coming, they pull apart, as if they weren't clasping hands.

The Boy keeps asking me what in the world I'm writing in my small book. But I don't tell him.

"You're writing, *Once upon a time there was a very stubborn rabbit.* Admit it," he says. I'm doing no such thing. And even if I were, that is the most hideous beginning of a tale I could ever imagine.

Sometimes the Sea asks me for a poem. I'm still not as good as she is, but I'm getting better with practice. I'll never be much of a rhymer, but just as there are different kinds of magic in the world, there are different kinds of poems, too.

Here is her favorite:

The Island of Hybrasil
Once it lived on every map,
drawn or painted,
just off the coast,
a roundish blob of an island.
Everyone knew of it,
until they didn't.
Until it disappeared into the sea—
vanishing from reality into imagination.
The last visitor found only
a castle,
a magician,
and four silver-gray rabbits.
Curious, those rabbits.
Unlikely seeds for an epic tale.

It isn't finished yet. And I'm not even sure if it's a poem, or perhaps the start of something different altogether. The Sea thinks it sounds more like a story, and that's just fine, she says. Stories and poems come from the same place.

It will probably take me a while to figure it all out.

But I've got time.

Author's Note

Hy-Brasil (also written as Ui Breasail) actually did appear on maps for hundreds of years, just off the western coast of Ireland. There are many legends that surround this mysterious island. It is said that Hy-Brasil only appears every seven years, that it is held down by four iron stakes at each corner, and that when those are removed, the island moves. Some legends claim that Hy-Brasil is the home of ancient Irish gods; others claim that the island is home to monks who preserved the records of an advanced society. But the story about Hy-Brasil that intrigued me the most was the 1674 report by Captain John Nesbit, who apparently visited Hy-Brasil and was greeted by a magician and some rather large rabbits.

Curious, those rabbits.

Sometimes that is all it takes for a story to bloom—a mystery, a legend, and a touch of something curious.

The story of Albie and her rabbit sisters grew from such seeds, but of course, all events and characters are pure fantasy, with a touch of historical inspiration. Albie's papa is based on decorated pilot Paddy Finucane, one of ten Irish pilots to fight in the Battle of Britain (although he was probably not married to a magical person). Barinthus, the sluagh, and the kelpies are all part of Celtic folklore.

As for the sea, well, anyone who has sat on a beach or a cliff and watched the hypnotic beauty of the waves or heard the poetry in the splashing of the surf knows that the sea's magic is real. I have tried to capture a small piece of her wonder on these pages.

Acknowledgments

Some books try to kill you when you're writing them. They make you wrestle each word onto the paper and wring the strength from your heart and soul, page by page by page.

Some books save you. They restore your trust in writing. In story. In yourself.

The Last Rabbit saved me. There are many thank-yous in order, for without this wonderful team, there would be no Albie. And at this point, I can't imagine a life without my little rabbit girl.

Thank you:

To Jordan Hamessley, my agent, who was the first official reader of the completed manuscript. Her love for Albie gave me faith in this book at a time I so desperately needed it. And to Jo Volpe, the amazing head of New Leaf Literary, who always, one hundred percent of the time, has my back.

To Dana Carey and Wendy Lamb, whose insight into EVERYTHING is something that I value beyond measure. These women. THESE WOMEN!! They are the kind of women Albie and her sisters aspire to be.

To everyone at Random House Children's Books who worked on *The Last Rabbit*. The author is not the only one who puts her heart and soul into a book. The behind-the-scenes team dedicate their lives to enriching the literary lives and imaginations of children everywhere. Without these folks there would be no books. Special thanks to designer Michelle Cunningham, managing editor Tamar Schwartz, copy editors Colleen Fellingham and Tricia Callahan, proofreader Annette Szlachta-McGinn, production manager Tracy Heydweiller, and everyone in marketing, publicity, and sales.

To Julie Mellan, whose illustrations captured the magic of the story and left tiny paw-prints on my heart.

To my parents, John and Nancy Moore, for believing.

To my sister, Susan Moore Daniels, and my brother, John Moore III, for standing by me through childhood and beyond.

To Kathy Duddy and Holly Pence, who remind me that family is more than blood.

To Chris Kopp and Nancy Villalobos, who read the first chapter long, long ago, and never forgot about a cantankerous little rabbit on a sinking island.

To the children of Jefferson Elementary School, who inspire me every day to be better.

And finally, to Noel, Issy, and Cali, the reasons I have any words to give. Despite how much I try to offer my books to this world as some sort of legacy, I know that they will never shine so bright as my girls.

About the Author

SHELLEY MOORE THOMAS grew up in New Mexico, the second of three children. A fan of fairy tales and UFOs, Shelley began channeling her abundant imagination toward writing back in elementary school. Now an elementary school teacher herself, Shelley spends her days helping the best people on the planet (children, of course!) unlock their creativity. Shelley lives in California with her kids and her dogs.

SHELLEYMOORETHOMAS.COM

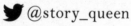 @story_queen

@storyqueen